That Kiss

"Love is the weather of life."

That Kiss in the Rain..

"Love is the weather of life."

Novoneel Chakraborty

Srishti
PUBLISHERS & DISTRIBUTORS

Sᴀɪsʜᴛɪ Pᴜʙʟɪsʜᴇʀs & Dɪsᴛʀɪʙᴜᴛᴏʀs
N-16, C. R. Park
New Delhi 110 019
srishtipublishers@gmail.com

First published by Srishti Publishers & Distributors in 2009
 6th impression, 2010
Copyright © Novoneel Chakraborty, 2009

Typeset in AGaramond 11pt. by Suresh Kumar Sharma at Srishti

Printed and bound in India

To all those *Angels* who saved my life on 14th April, 2008·
at 4:05 pm, precisely.

Acknowledgment

During the writing process one thinks only he is in control but after a book gets completed and one looks back, he knows it wouldn't have been possible without the presence of few important people.

Special and heartfelt thanks to:

My family (parents and *didi*). Without you all I am just a black and white rainbow.

My late grandfather. For expressing yourself through me. I *feel* the warmth of your guiding hand on me whenever I write.

My friends. For being a constant source of support.

Publisher. For guiding me towards the right path. I just love the discussions I have with you.

Prologue

14th April.

Sometime in future.

"Is there any festival which can be celebrated every day and not once a year?" Asked the girl.

"Wait till you fall in love with me." Replied the boy.

THE STORM WAS BRUTALLY VIOLENT. And the sea, hypnotized by the storm's spirit, had also gone insane. Random lightning appeared as evil chuckles of destiny on the pitch-dark face of the sky while the echo of thunders that followed seemed to carry the etiquette of her once said words.

Everything's easy. If you are in love – really in love – every goddamn thing is easy. Perhaps as easy as giving in to fate often is.

The man was completely at the mercy of the wild sea and the ravaging storm. Together they stood between him and his destination. In a desperate attempt to steady his position, he looked around for help and in doing so heard the sky resound, once again, with a thunder.

Hundred times you have told me why you love me but do you know why I love you? I love you because you do to my life what I myself would have done had it been under my control.

That was what he was looking for – control – and that, like Jerry does with Tom, was eluding him. Somehow he managed to latch onto the ridges of the boat knowing well it was only a temporary solution. For a moment he wondered what made him dare the journey. Why did she go away? They were quite happy with each other. He soon discarded the thought. When one is in a storm there's no time for any *what* or *why*. Survival, at times, is freedom itself.

In the doom-inspiring night he was sure of only one thing: he had to reach her quickly. For the air, carrying the haunting notes from the flute of fate, told him time was running out. He swallowed a lump. A decision was imminent. He looked around. Nothing encouraged what his heart demanded of him. Yet he stood up, balanced himself uncomfortably on the ever so whirling boat and jumped.

Though the sea was still wild he had faith in its waves and that it would, in the end – out of sympathy, empathy or whatever –take him to her; never mind the course. But the moment he surrendered himself to the sea, its huge waves, exuding a giggle, took the boat away much faster than expected. Trapped? A bolt of thunder called for his attention again.

Love is the reason to remain sane all life and yet it is an excuse to be insane in all the moments that make up a life.

Each time the titanic waves swallowed him, it took a valiant effort to resurface and breathe normally. Plenty of water had already gone in and he could sense his surrender weighing on his limbs and lungs.

This is life sweetheart! You, me and our moments.

The thunder, whenever it called out, escalated his urge to fight. The ticking seconds stretched his might and pushed his will but every try, every attempt and every will fell short of the power of the foe. His ears had, by now, been blocked and the lungs too experienced an increase in the traffic of water. He repeatedly raised his hand, though irresolutely, appealing to nature. But every quest of his was ruthlessly overruled. Then came a wave – the most gigantic of all – and ingested him such that he was hurled into a catacomb of broken dreams, lost times and abandoned happiness. Every sound, apart from a distant tintinnabulation, diminished. It slowly ascended at first – the tintinnabulation – and then attained a stasis. Everything before him seemed milk white. He heard a voice next.

"How are you feeling?"

He tried, budging uncomfortably on the bed, but couldn't see anything.

"Nothing to worry about. Everything's under control." The heinous truth hid well behind the warmth in the voice.

"But" The jaws hurt. After an anticipating pause he spoke slowly, "Why are my eyes...band...?" He couldn't finish.

"They aren't bandaged. Try opening them slowly."

He did. The vision was blurry at first and then, as experience does to life, sequaciously became distinct. He tried to move but an excruciating pain in his muscles held him back.

"The doctor said it might pain for few more days."

He looked at the person. *Why is he caring so much for me?*

"You don't know how happy and relieved I am now." The man rubbed his eyes. "I thought you wouldn't –"

"Who are you?" He cut him short.

And his best friend of twenty-six years kept looking at him in utter bewilderment.

PALLAVI

The drug was showing its effect. And as he stumbled out of the pub they too were on their feet.

The three of them followed him to the lobby of the five-star hotel and with a mask of indifference accompanied him into the elevator. He moved out on the third floor while they stepped out on the fourth. By the time he reached his room, at the end of the posh corridor, the team of three had already climbed down a floor using the stairs. As they closed in on the man they saw him fidgeting with the doorknob. One of the three walked ahead and helped him with the knob. As the door opened the guy collapsed on the floor like a lump of meat. By then the other two had joined the first and they locked the door from inside.

One of the girls pulled out the biscuit-shaped key ring dangling shamelessly from the man's jeans and swiped it on the desired spot beside the door. The entire room was instantly educated with light.

"Light is done." Said the first girl.

"Camera?" Asked the second one.

A while later the third one spoke ready with her latest Sony Erickson mobile, "Action!"

Her friends, holding the man's arms, dragged him to the centre of the room. The man, though conscious, didn't know what exactly was happening to or with him.

"What's up?" He somehow mumbled.

"You had a minor accident. But don't you worry. We three nurses shall take care of you." With the drug commanding his senses, the man thought the words were Gospel. He closed his eyes praying for a quick recovery. Next, one of the girls undid his belt and the other dragged down his jeans. The third one had her mobile phone's camera on pointing towards the target. The succeeding seconds saw the underwear, too, being tugged down mercilessly.

"I hope he doesn't live his life dick-size!" The girls abhorred the sight.

For a while everything from the guy's face to his toe was recorded and then the camera was smartly switched off.

"Was that a necessity?"

"If he recognizes us then we got to have something to shut him up."

"Alright, let's repeat ourselves."

"Four inches." The first girl raised her hand.

"Five and a half inches." The sight had murdered the second girl's confidence.

"Three and a half inches." The third beamed with a winner's attitude.

The first girl took out her belt which had measurements printed on it and bent down facing the man's groin. She took his limp tool in one hand and held her belt against it. With a gloomy face she declared, "Three and a half inches."

Pallavi punched the air in joy.

"What the fuck is this? Did you do this guy before?"

"Me? With Mr. three and a half inches? Correct your sanity sweetheart. But before that give me the bucks I deserve." The losers took out thousand rupees each and handed it to the winner. Pallavi took the crispy currency notes in her hand and said, "There's only one way you can beat Pallavi." The other two looked at her directly as she put the money in her pocket. "If you have her permission!"

It was four in the morning when Pallavi unlocked her one-bedroom rented flat in Vasant Vihar, Delhi. Her gait, after consuming a bottle of Orange Twist, two Tequila shots and some Martini, resembled that of her life's – wayward and unsure. The main door, because of the closer, locked itself comfortably as Pallavi stumbled across the room and collapsed on the floor. With heavy eyes and senses mislead by alcohol she crawled the rest of the distance to reach her bed. After climbing on it she carelessly spread her hands, wide, and lay assuming the shape of Christ nailed on a cross. Her hips, coincidentally, rested on the remote control and the television was switched on.

The repeat telecast of one of the daily soaps, in a leading entertainment channel, was on air. A man was, supposedly, leaving his wife who, like a crazy spirit hoping to come back to life soon, held onto him. There was also a baby who was shot from various angles each time with a thunderous background score. And because the television was wired with a woofer thus the entire room started bouncing the baby's cry.

Though Pallavi was in a no man's land between sleep and reality the baby's cry hit her ears sharply and subsequently made her mind face a nostalgic kaleidoscope. Once upon a time she was a kid too…she must have cried as well…but why didn't her parents take care of her? All she ever wanted was her parents understanding her without the medium of language but …was it asking too much? Why didn't she get to her first love before the other girl did? Of all the men she had in her life why didn't anyone arouse her innocence the way he did?

She could hear the television baby cry but any differentiation – as to whether she herself was a recently turned twenty-seven year old sexy spinster or a two-year-old kid, crying for food – seemed impossible.

The night was sadistic but the wind it brought along was worse. Together they rocked the hut which its owner and his wife had carefully built with stolen pieces of brick from a nearby construction site.

A bamboo barrier dissected the hut. One side was a music instrument repair shop and the other housed six people – two adults and four kids with their empty-stomach dreams.

On the business side, Manohar Nehra was tightening the last screws of an archaic Harmonium while on the hope side his wife, Sharda, was finishing the last bunch of paper packets which were scheduled to be delivered to the shops around the locality early morning. Her workaholic hands were also making sure the kids slept tight – without being influenced by the roaring wind outside – by caressing their innocuous foreheads, which, she thought, had invisible impressions of their doomed fate, every ten minutes.

"*Kya kehti ho?*" Manohar wanted to know his wife's mind. Though Sharda heard every word distinctly but chose not to respond. She looked at her kids instead. The first three were boys and the fourth was a year old girl. Her eyes remained fixed on her. The baby had gone to sleep on her own after crying all evening for food. Sharda's guilt was on the verge of assuming the role of tears when she heard her husband speak, "*Maine pucha tum kya kehti ho?*"

"*Jaisi aapki marzi.*" She knew her opinion never mattered. And sometimes the only option one has is to haplessly watch destiny take its own course. Doesn't matter the pain. Doesn't matter the emotions. Doesn't matter what one actually deserves…or thinks he does.

The proposal of two lakh rupees cash in exchange of their girl came from a middle man named Jagat. He had his liaison with many orphanages and frequently struck deals between the needy – one in need of a child and the other in need of money – with fifty percent of the pecuniary involved being his commission.

Jagat happened to notice the Vimani family coming out of several orphanages each time without a smile. In the end it was outside the main gate of Sunrise Orphanage when Jagat offered them his service.

"The health and background of the baby is my responsibility."

The Vimani couple looked at each other. "At least you can have a look." Jagat insisted and a day later they decided to check the baby out.

Sharda used to deliver paper packets to Jagat's brother's shop as well. And once, when he saw Sharda come to his shop with her daughter, Sarita, he knew his brother would be interested. It didn't take Jagat long to convince Prakash Vimani about two lakhs. But what took time was preparing Manohar and Sharda for the deal.

"Just imagine one lakh rupees!" Jagat was at his con-best. "Not only will it take care of your boys' education but will also give you a chance to start your own small business if you please. Moreover your nod to the deal will allow your only daughter to live as a queen; won't you do this much for her?"

When Prakash and Shobha Vimani saw Sarita – smiling and eagerly trying to touch everything within her reach – their desire of having a baby was underlined. After Prakash's doctor declared Sarita medically fit he gave the money to Jagat and took the baby home.

Within a week a grand party was organised in the Vimani house and a new name was chosen for the girl. Pallavi Vimani.

Sarita's train of life started to chug forward only after she became Pallavi. Though she herself was unaware of the motion but that is probably God's exclusive gift for kids: bliss in the form of innocence.

What Pallavi got from Prakash and Shobha, in addition to the sempiternal love and emotional care which even her biological parents had given her, was the best brands of clothing from whichever mall they went to, whatever toys and dolls she pointed her little fingers at and whichever cake, pastry or chocolates she stared at for more than five seconds. The maid on whose lap she cried once was never seen in the house again. The last week of every third month they went holidaying and by the time Pallavi was eleven she alone could give all the tourist guides, from Kashmir to Kanyakumari and from Kutch to Kolkata, serious professional competition.

From the time Prakash put her in one of the leading schools of Delhi, Pallavi's congenital intelligence came to the foreground. She never sat and studied in one place but whenever it was results time, she stood only one place; *numero uno*. Same was true for her artistic and sporting endeavours. There was no devotion but whenever in a competition Pallavi invariably edged the others out because of which no one ever cared to tell her the importance of preparation.

And just when her ignorant age convinced her that she had experienced everything in life, that she was unbeatable and whatever was left of life would only bore her, something refreshingly new happened. Pallavi, for the first time, fell in love.

It was her best friend's birthday party. Pallavi, to begin with, was enjoying a lot playing pass-the-puzzle, *antakshari,* dumb-charade and other games. There were two persons playing the role of jokers who were also responsible for a constant smile on everyone's face. Finally the candles were blown off and the birthday cake was cut to a stentorian clap with a happy-birthday-to-you perched on every child's lips.

After finishing with one round of vegetarian delicacies Pallavi decided to try some non vegetarian ones and thus proceeded towards the buffet corner. After filling her plate sufficiently she was walking back to her seat when she discovered it had already been occupied. Panning her eyes quickly Pallavi noticed, with a riled expression, no other seat was available.

"I was sitting here." She said looking straight at the boy, ready for any retort from him. *I have handled so many like him in school*, she thought.

The boy looked lost for a while and then replied softly, "I am sorry. I didn't know you were sitting here." He got up and walked away. *No fight back? Good for him!* Though Pallavi got her seat but her eyes, as if filming him, kept the boy at its focus. He looked cute and for girls of her age that's the most intoxicating feature in a boy. She saw him going to every corner of the room in search of a seat but in vain.

Something inside her – seeing the boy helpless in his attempt – felt diluted. She walked up to the boy and said, "You can sit there."

"But you were sitting there."

"I don't wish to anymore." Pallavi went to the other room and all the time, while having dinner, kept observing the boy from the corner of the curtain. And later that night when she slept on her cozy bed hugging Nonu, her favourite king size teddy, Pallavi dreamt the exact scene shown in a romantic film a day before. Only that the roles were played by her and the boy she met at the party.

"Who is he?" Pallavi asked Shweta. Together they were looking at Shweta's birthday photographs.

"The one in green?"

"No!" Pallavi used her finger this time. "This one…the one in black."

"Oh! He is Dino."

"Never saw him around before."

"Ya he shifted to our neighborhood couple of months back. Our parents know each other." Shweta suddenly frowned and looked at Pallavi. "Wait a minute…are you repenting you haven't seen him before?"

"No!" Pallavi said and blushed.

Whenever she saw her friends talking to boys in the class or during interval or even after school Pallavi wondered what fun it would have been if Dino and she studied in the same school. She even made up her mind for a switch but when her parents refused to give in to her silly reasons Pallavi reluctantly forgot about the matter.

This, though, did not affect the silent confessions she made and the sublime realizations that happened to her day and night. And three months later God, out of respect for the several undefined cravings boiling inside her innocuous heart with the bubbles of first love, granted Pallavi her wish.

Shweta and Dino, as per their parents' wish, had started taking tuition for mathematics at her place. The moment Shweta told Pallavi about it she immediately made sure her mathematics tutor got chucked out and within two days she was at Shweta's place eager to know more about the additions and multiplications of love.

The two hours of tuition, in a way, was boring because Pallavi grasped all the concepts and the theorems quicker than both Shweta and Dino. But this fact, being a blessing, helped her observe Dino more and more. She used to arrive an hour early hoping to catch up with Dino but as it turned out he was a punctuality freak and almost always dropped in a minute before their teacher came.

After the tuitions they chatted for a while amongst themselves but whenever Shweta tried to play the cupid and someway thought of leaving her friend alone with Dino, he came up with an excuse to leave. And everyday in school Pallavi had the same set of questions for Shweta:

Did he enquire about me?

Did you tell him anything about me?

Do you think he looked at me a little differently yesterday?

Do you think he might be interested in me?

Did he appreciate my dress?

And to go with the quotidian queries were only one answer: No!

Five months passed by and Pallavi could do nothing about her feelings. All she remained was Dino's tuition friend. Just like Shweta is, she rebuked herself and cried. There was something that wasn't letting her come out with the proposal herself. Guys do that, she had seen in the movies. And going by her parent's feedback she was a princess who could only forward her hand to a prince who was ready to get down on his knees for her. But why doesn't he reciprocate? Her tears asked her heart but the latter had only one answer: patience.

The day, when time chose to wipe the mist of confusion from the surface of her mind, started strangely for Pallavi. She was gripped by an excruciating pain in her lower abdomen. Though she went to school but was forced to come back home during the interval. The pain, with the day's progress, escalated further and in the end she had to, for the first time, forgo the mathematics tuition as well. In the evening Shweta called up.

"Have you been to the doctor?"

"Yes." Pallavi was on her bed. "He gave few shit medicines. Yuck! But forget that…tell me anything happened today?"

There was silence.

"Hello?"

"Ya."

"Anything happened today?"

"No, sir only gave us the previous day's -"

"You know I am not asking about that."

Silence again.

"What's the matter with you? I am in pain and you are behaving weird!"

"Dino talked about you."

"Really?" Pallavi sat up instantly with a fresh brio. "What did he say?"

"He said you look like his girl friend."

It took Pallavi seven hours to react to the fact that Dino was seriously committed to another girl. And when she did it was in the form of torrential amount of tears. The sky of her emotions, it seemed, was adamant to fill up the craters formed by destiny. Much like the way water bodies came up on Earth to give it a fine balance. Only this time, perhaps, the purpose wasn't solved.

How can he have a girl friend and how can they possibly be committed? I am sure I fell in love with him first so he is only mine!

After a trivial dinner the pain in her lower abdomen turned acute again. As she cried profusely she wondered which tear was the effect of which pain. An hour later Pallavi felt a strong urge to go to the loo. She got up, with a facial expression tantamount to a crunched leaf, and went right in. She tugged down her undergarment and was stiff with shock. A thin line of blood trickled down her inner thighs. *What's happening?* She wanted to call her mother but the excruciating pain, instead, made her lock her jaws and sit down on the floor pressing her abdomen.

Little Pallavi, as the pain extorted more tears, realized one important thing: loving someone truly is dangerous because it makes one bleed from the most private part.

HAASIL

"Lup-dup, lup-dup, lup-dup goes the heart. Every dup in my heart is because of the lup in yours. And every lup of your heart is because of the dup in mine. Such is the connection of love."

He could – from the time his senses came to life in the hospital – hear the words echoing softly within the realm of his sub-conscious. He talked less but thought a lot. And when he was discharged from the hospital, a month later, things only added to his confusion.

The garden, the main door, the servant, the hall room, the steps to his bedroom, the bed, the bath tub and every other thing in the house gave him a déjà vu feeling but the problem was, nothing triggered any nostalgia. There was also a feminine energy all over the place. It was feminine because it imbued within him a feeling that life, with all its flaws, was still worth a try. And only a *she* can make a *he* feel that way.

Apart from lying on bed, from Sun to Moon, there wasn't much for Haasil to do. The accident part was evident to him while the memory lapse portion was relayed in a mild manner.

"The doctor said it'll take some time before you remember everything." Nitin told him.

And whenever the stream of sedative, injected by Jennifer, the full-time deployed nurse at his house, mixed with his busy river of blood, a different world opened up.

A faceless woman…a faceless man…walking hand in hand beside a seashore… sometimes kissing sometimes only hugging…cuddled together – their jaded and naked bodies wrapped with a white satin bed sheet – on the terrace of a palatial house facing a sunrise…flowers…chocolates…clicks of camera and to go with it sounds of laughter…a candle lit dinner…the clasping of hands followed by some romantic promises…sessions of passionate love making...a Lucullan marriage ceremony...the blessings and good wishes...then a drive on a long road...and then...nothing...

Haasil, lying sideways, looked out of one of the windows that framed a page of the sky with small paragraphs of black clouds.

After almost an hour, gaping indolently at the sky, Haasil got up. The moment he was on his feet the sky belched with a thunder. Rain was only a matter of time.

Haasil limped, to start with, and then ambled forward to reach the window. There was no one in sight. Couple of auto rickshaws passed by and then, as was imminent, it started raining. A wet smell of the soil impregnated the air and inhaling it he closed his eyes. When he opened them he saw two figures – a girl and a boy – standing, face to face, on the middle of the road getting drenched in the rain. A faint smile flexed his cheeks. His engrossment didn't allow him to see a car approaching the couple. When, in the next second, he did see it a knot formed in his stomach. He wanted to scream, shout and yell at the couple to alert them. But nothing came out as fear locked the voluntariness of all his senses. And before he could do anything the car smashed the couple. *Shit!* In the next instant, though, he saw them standing as they were before, unharmed. The car had gone through them! Haasil closed his eyes tight, for once, and then opened them again. Neither the car was there nor the couple. *What the hell is happening?* He rubbed his eyes and looked at the wet street again. This time the girl had her arms around the boy's neck and was standing on her toe to reach his lips.

God bless them! Haasil smiled. But within the next blink the couple vanished again. Vexed, he slowly walked back and ensconced on his bed.

A gush of wind, through the carelessly ajar window, broke into the room and pushed the door of the adjacent wardrobe squeezing out a soft squeak. For a moment he kept looking at the wardrobe. Though he was in his own house, Haasil wondered, still he didn't have a clue to what it actually contained. The next instance he thought of opening the wardrobe.

There were many shirts, pants and few suits along with – Haasil observed closely – some gorgeous sarees, exquisite chikan embroidered salwar suits and few classy gowns. He was about to call the nurse when something lying in-between the clothes, on one of the shelves, caught his eye. He took it in his hands. The gold coloured and delicately designed frame contained the picture of a couple. Haasil, with the frame in his hand, moved in front the mirror adjacent to the wardrobe. He looked at the man smiling in the photograph once and then at the mirror. He recognized himself. *But who is this lady? Is she…my wife?*

"Jennifers." He called out. Some urgent footsteps stamped the staircase and a second later the nurse appeared. "What are you doing standing?" She was gasping for air, "You should be on the bed. Please."

"Can you get me to Nitin?"

"Sure but please sit down first." She helped Haasil get to the bed. He kept gaping at the photograph while the nurse got busy dialing Nitin's number from the cordless phone kept on the nearby dressing table.

"Nitin sir is on the line." She gave the phone to Haasil.

"Hello."

"Haasil? Anything's the problem?"

"I got a photo frame inside my wardrobe. There is a woman with me. Who is she?"

"How come you opened the wardrobe? What is the nurse doing?"

"*Who* is she Nitin?"

"She is…" *shit, I can't lie about this. I dare not.* "She is your wife."

"My wife? What's her name?"

"Palki."

"Palki?" There was a pause. "Where is she? Doesn't she know about my accident?"

"She is in the States right now."

"States? As in United States of America?

"Ya."

"What is she doing there?"

"Studying at the University of Wisconsin."

"Does she know about my accident?"

"No."

"No? Didn't she inquire where I was all these days? Doesn't she care-?"

"No! It's nothing like that. What I meant was she knows about your accident and also the fact that you are on bed rest. That's why-"

"That's why what?"

"That's why" there was no scope for any second thought, "She is eager to come to India next week." *How? I don't know,* Nitin thought and added, "But I don't know she'll get lucky with the tickets or not."

"I want to talk to her now."

"Now?" Nitin swallowed a lump.

"Ya now. Any problem?"

"Listen buddy let me come over to your place and I'll explain the situation to you."

"Explain which situation?"

"I got to be there in front of you for this one."

"Is everything alright with her?" The voice reflected genuine concern.

"Ya." It was a soft reply. *I hate lying like this.* "Ya. Everything's fine."

This time Nitin was more convincing.

"Okay. So when are you coming here?"

"ASAP!" *Christ, kill me before I reach him.*

"I'll wait." Haasil ended the call and gave the phone back to Jennifer.

He stretched himself straight on the bed holding the photo frame. As he saw Jennifer leaving the room Haasil opened the frame and took the picture out. One at a time he observed Palki's features: the eyes, eye brows, nose, lips, smile and he finally concluded: *I am a lucky man.*

Smiling to himself he flipped the photograph on an impulse only to find something written on it…

Our story began not when we came into each other's life. It began from the time when life happened to us. We are not only made for each other but were thought for each other too.

"Good afternoon sir." Instead of Raghu *chacha*, the regular servant, Jennifer opened the door.

"Good afternoon." Nitin responded with indifference. "How is he?"

"Fine. He has just had his lunch."

Without caring to converse further Nitin headed for the stairs and, climbing two steps at a time, reached his best friend's room in no time.

"How are you doing *dost*?" Nitin quickly pulled up a chair from a corner near the bed and sat on it, legs crossed.

Haasil looked at him for a while and then said, "Better."

"Just a matter of few more months and-"

"Can you please clarify what exactly happened with me?"

"I have told you already. You met with a bad accident."

"Ya, but where?"

"On way from Bangalore."

"Why was I there?"

"You – you were there for some business work." It was a lie.

Haasil was pensive for some time and then queried again, "Was I alone?"

Avoid the truth as long as possible, Nitin recollected the doctor's words.

"Ya."

"And how did you find me?"

"A family was driving by the accident spot. They cared to stop by and also happened to get hold of your cell that – thank God – was still working. They called up the last caller – that was me! – and then took you to a nearby nursing home from where – after I joined them – we shifted you to Lilavati."

Seconds became minutes but neither spoke a word. And when they did, it happened together.

"Do-" "You-"

Nitin gestured to Haasil to carry on.

"You were talking about a situation over phone. What is it?"

Nitin first cleared his throat slightly and then started, "Palki knows about your accident. But she is yet to know about your head injuries and what it has done to you. You understand?"

After staring for a few seconds Haasil nodded.

"And now if you talk to her and she happens to guess the situation – what happens? She'll know obviously – I don't know how she'll react."

"You said she'll be here next week."

Nitin licked his lips nervously. "She might be." *She never will...* "If she gets the ticket that is."

"What is it with the ticket? Is all of America flying down to India?"

"No, but these days they have become stricter and-"

"Anyways, tell me a little about us. I mean Palki and me."

"What all do you want to know?"

"You know, from the time I saw her photo in the morning till now I have been infuriated with myself. Here is a woman who is supposed to be my wife and also loves me very much..." Haasil glanced at Nitin for confirmation who responded quickly with a thumbs-up gesture. "And here I am" Haasil continued, "trying to guess everything about her. Guessing things about my wife? This is bullshit! Honestly, are you sure I'll really remember all of it...one day...any day?"

It looks like a temporary retrograde Amnesia case. Nothing concrete can be said as of now, the doctor had said. Though Nitin nodded yes but with locked jaws.

Haasil sighed in relief. "I want you to help me out."

"Always."

"I don't know when she'll get her ticket but I would like to talk to her before that." Haasil's eyes were locked with Nitin's.

"Sure." Nitin was the first to turn away.

"In that case I neither want to suffer any embarrassment nor do I want her to know I don't remember her as such. I hope you understand my..." Haasil didn't complete.

Nitin thought for a while and said, "I do." He took his mobile phone out, switched it off and then looking at his friend, said, "Alright. Let me tell you about your life..."

PALLAVI

Control – Pallavi's adolescence helped her infer from her friends' screw-ups and break-offs – was one single thing that every woman should stick to. If she loses control over anything but more importantly over the species from Mars, she loses her significance altogether.

With the coming of sexy sixteen Pallavi discovered better things about her gender. When her mother, for the first time, gave her a proper brassiere to wear Pallavi was ecstatically curious. She went straight to the bathroom, stripped herself and tried the new piece of clothing which her mother said would be with her longer than any of her best friends.

As Pallavi stood naked in front of the full-length mirror she observed all the developments carefully. The once-upon-a-time chest now resembled two airtight pouches of milk. She squeezed them hard and smiled as a response to the erotic tickle it generated. The chocolate colored nipples, that stood out on her breasts, stiffened reacting to her finger's soft caress. She also tried, without once averting her eyes from the mirror, to pose like the models of those sex magazines that she noticed from the corner of her eyes each time she, along with her friends, passed by the roadside stall near her school. At first she cupped her breasts and pouted her lips. *Sexy!* Next, Pallavi turned around and put both her hands on the clothes rack above to have a look at her bare back. *Sexier!* Once again she cupped her breasts, positioned sideways and broke her spine a little jutting out her hips in the process. *Sexiest!*

While taking bath the water – trickling down the mountains, valleys and plateaus epitomizing her body – imbued strange kinds of emotion within her. As if something urgently wanted to come out from her deepest within. But when it didn't the weather of frustration ruled the rest of her bath. Later, while blow drying her hair, the hair-dryer sparked an idea in her mind.

She stealthily took the dryer to the bathroom, plugged it in, stripped her lowers and then slowly brought the machine near her abdomen. She spread her legs further and placed the dryer between her legs. As the air from it kissed her most private corner a moan came out. The feeling was heaven! With eyes closed and mind lost in some far away land Pallavi kept moving the drier up, down and circular. Sometimes she closed in and at times kept the machine at a distance from her pleasure gate. Though initially she saw Dino's face but then Leonardo di Caprio took over and exactly four minutes later, when she cared to touch her vagina, she was amazed not only by its wetness but also how satisfied the process had made her. As if frustration was liquid in state. And a little thick too, a quick finger-analysis told her.

Sitting on the smooth tiled floor, in an overtly relaxed demeanor, Pallavi had a premonition. Her life, after the sublime serendipity, would surely witness a rebellion from the plethora of alien emotions the dryer introduced her to. There was also a hint of disappointment because it took sixteen years for her senses to tour the amative gardens inside her. But Pallavi knew, as her lips stretched with a naughty smile, a sexual renaissance was inevitable now, for a girl was about to become a woman.

Pallavi learnt more about a man's body – with delicious, and sometimes scary, length and thickness – after she entered the word 'sex' on a search engine and perused the pictures and videos in the websites that followed up. And steadily she became an ace on the subject.

Her new Biology teacher in school, was a touch apprehensive about teaching the chapter on Human Reproduction.

"This" She looked at the class, "Is the male reproductive organ." She turned to the next chart, "And this is the female reproductive organ. It opens to-"

"What's inside it ma'am?" A boy shot the question.

"I know!" Even before the teacher could reply Pallavi raised her hand. And as the teacher glanced at her she stood up.

"It's called the Gräfenberg spot or popularly G-Spot. It's that zone in a female's pussy which, if stimulated, arouses her like a crazy bitch and helps her reach screaming orgasms."

The students gaped at Pallavi who was looking, gleefully, at the teacher who, in turn, was standing jaw-dropped.

The porn sites convinced Pallavi it was smart on God's part to make a woman multi-orgasmic. We bleed once a month but can enjoy for much longer than guys, she thought. *Oh! I'll take that any day!*

Though her academics suffered but Pallavi didn't let her status drop below average. She studied till midnight and then till late in the morning remained on the Internet. Chatting became her obsession. She used to log on to Yahoo Messenger first, then to her favourite room and in the end invariably found some guy who, being at the zenith of sexual frustration, was ready to open everything up at the slightest provocation.

Hotdude143: Hi babe! A-S-L?

Sweetgal: Hi. 25-female-India. Yours?

Hotdude143: 26-male-India. Want to chat hot?

Sweetgal: Sure! You got a webcam?

Hotdude143: Ya you?

Sweetgal: Ya but I want to see you first.

Hotdude143: You promise you'll show yourself?

Sweetgal: Oh yes but first you.

The boy positioned his web cam in a manner that showed him neck downwards. He stripped himself slowly and within few seconds stood naked in front of the cam.

Hotdue143: Like wat u c?

Sweetgal: Ya. Turn around.

He did.

Sweetgal: I like ur ass.

Hotdude143: U like my dick?

Sweetgal: Not bad. Can u jerk it 4 me?

He complied while Pallavi sat with her hair drier. They came together.

Hotdude143: Now ur turn babe.

And all he saw, on the right hand bottom corner of his computer screen, was: sweetgal just logged out.

She did the same with Hotman, Citydude, Midnight Gigolo and the like. Manipulating boys' mind to turn them into craving sexual slaves became her favourite sport and aphrodisiac.

"Have you heard of *Ponceo*?" Pallavi asked her group as they were ambling towards the canteen during interval.

"Is that the latest sex pose?" The group shared a hearty laugh.

"I was in my aunt's place at Chile with my parents this summer. There I had gone to a pub where teenagers like us were trying *Ponceo*."

"Oh it's a drug!" Ankita quipped.

"No duffer." Pallavi hit her softly. "Ponceo is an honor given to the one who pairs up the most."

"Did you also join?"

"Join?" Pallavi widened her eyes, "I got the title baby!" She lied with confidence.

"How many guys did you pair up with?"

"Twenty five." The words were coated with pride.

"Is there any difference between Indian guys and the locals there?"

"Not really. Here they ask your name then date and there they date first and then, if necessary, ask your name." She winked.

Soon the girls came across one of their classmates sitting alone inside the canteen.

"Hey Mitika!" The girls joined her, "What's up?"

"Nothing." Her face read otherwise. Realizing it, her friends sat beside her.

"Give us the truth." Pallavi demanded.

Mitika, for once, looked up and then started sobbing. "I love Rahul a lot. Couple of weeks ago I had confessed my love to him. And he had reciprocated too. Last week after tuitions while we were coming back we got a little intimate."

"Describe the little."

"We smooched and also touched each other all over."

"And from the next day Rahul is ignoring you, right?"

Mitika gaped at Pallavi, rubbed her eyes and asked, "How do you know?"

"Never mind! But if you want I can bring Rahul back on track." She looked at everyone in the group, "Latest by early next week."

"How will you do that?"

"I'll," her eyes twinkled, "Only request him."

Rahul – to the girls with the right hormonal changes – was a stud. He was rich: that made him desirable; he was handsome: that made him irresistible; he was a flirt: that made him popular. Though he made his dates feel special like a melody does to lyrics but on a personal level, Rahul thought of girls and forwarded SMSes alike: Read them, enjoy them and lastly delete them in case they mess up your inbox.

Since Pallavi was one of a kind in Rahul's batch, and school, who always remained indifferent to his lover boy fame thus it made her his favourite fantasy. Whenever he masturbated, as a reflex to watching porn flicks, Rahul's mind easily swapped the faces of the porn stars with Pallavi's and his. The fervour infused within the vividness of it was evident in the amount of discharge thereafter.

When Jatin, a good friend, informed Rahul about Pallavi gaping at him during classes he felt his balls gravid with an amorous ambition. And when Pallavi came up to him during a basketball session, he realized his friend was spot on.

"Hi!" Pallavi's voice was soaked in seduction.

"Hi." Rahul turned to her after scoring a basket for his team.

"I love the way you play." The last word was stressed. *Which game is she talking about?* Rahul thought.

"Will you teach me too?" The seduction gave way to a tease.

"Sure!"

For the three days that followed they practiced basketball – only the two of them – after school. Lift your heels a little – he showed her – and keep your waist – he touched them properly – straight. Hold the ball without any strain in your hands – he was behind her feeling her round hips on his pelvis – and then scoop it towards the basket with ease! As the ball entered the basket and popped out from below, Rahul cried out, "That's how you score!"

Pallavi only nodded in appreciation.

That night, after exchanging their phone numbers, they talked till early morning. Everything, from criticizing their teachers to the latest film gossips to each other's past crushes to the concept of love and lastly the other's opinion on sex, was covered.

"Have you ever experienced cyber sex?" Rahul put it straight.

"No, what's that?" Pallavi faked innocence.

After Rahul told her about what she already knew Pallavi gave her consent to experience it with him.

The following night both of them logged onto the messenger on time.

Playboy666: Hi Pallavi! Rahul here.

Sweetgal: Hi! How are you?

Playboly666: I am fine. Should we start?

Sweetgal: Sure!!! But you remember our deal?

Playboy666: Ya! Today it's my turn and tomorrow yours. Are you ready baby?

Sweetgal: Give me a minute!

Pallavi quickly clicked on the icon of the software that helped record webcam content.

Sweetgal: Now am ready!

The show started. Though it happened slowly but once Rahul was completely naked things began to move on. She made him masturbate on cam, pose like a dog, tie his hands and behave as a sex slave and slap his own ass while pole dancing. And each time his sexual urges, along with Pallavi's carnal requests, fell a notch below on the scale of decadence Rahul couldn't believe his good luck. By the time the online saga ended Rahul was drained of energy.

Sweetgal: That was great! See you tomorrow.

Pallavi, immediately after logging out, first converted the recorded video into .3gp format and then downloaded it onto her mobile phone.

Next day during interval Pallavi, partnered with Mitika, walked up to Rahul and showed him the recording.

"What the fuck is this?"

"Arabian Night."

The girls – as the video played on – watched Rahul intently.

"Either you accept Mitika as your girlfriend or this video is going on a Dandi march."

"I don't believe this shit. You bitch...I'll report to the principal...you'll pay for this." He was fuming.

"Right now you don't have that option."

Rahul thought for a while with his expression changing from that of a wounded tiger to a trapped deer.

"O-okay."

"Good. So Mitika here's your boy friend."

Mitika, stepping up to Rahul, slapped him hard. His jaws dropped open. *This isn't happening to me. No way!*

"I don't want a dog as my boy friend." Mitika roared and walked off. Pallavi – all smiles – helped Rahul close his mouth. "Poor Mr. *Poop-ular.*" Apart from his ears everything seemed out of order.

"I hope now he stops being a MOMO." He heard the girls in the distance.

"MOMO?"

"Ho*mo*sexual *M*otherfucker."

"But how can a guy be both a homo and a motherfucker at the same time?"

"Oh! You never know guys!" Pallavi concluded.

Life, till tenth grade, was like a nappy, exciting within her a carefree attitude. But during twelfth grade it became a sanitary napkin gripping Pallavi with insecurity. Unlike her friends she didn't have any futuristic career goal. *One monster at a time*, was her rule. And the first one was called Board Exams.

She became aware of the syllabus only a week before the exams were scheduled to begin. And in doing so a truth dawned on her: *even if I study non-stop till my first exam still I won't be able to complete it*. In the end Pallavi chose to study smart instead of hard. She discussed the subjects with her teachers and also batch mates, the ones who ranked, and made a list according to importance. She studied whatever she could but, one day before the exam when she realized it wasn't enough, photographed the rest of the pages. Next, she loaded it on her father's mobile and took it with her to the exam venue.

"Hey Pallavi! What happened?" Every one had the same query seeing her wearing a neck collar.

"Just my bad luck. Twisted my neck a day before yesterday. God is so cruel. Don't know how I'll write my exams."

Exactly after one hour Pallavi excused herself to the toilet. There, she opened her neck collar which was hiding the mobile, switched it on and carefully absorbed the points in the photographed pages. This went on for every exam till the last day came and Pallavi came out of the room without the collar.

"Hey what happened? Suddenly you are alright?"

"I told you God is cruel. He made me experience the pain only during exams." She didn't stop for any reactions.

The school farewell night was arranged exactly a week after the exams were over. Since the time she witnessed her senior's farewell party – a year back – Pallavi had started lusting for the Miss Agnes School title. But there was competition. *I like competition as it's only fair to give others a chance to lose*, she pepped herself. And in the last one year she zeroed in on three potential competitors.

When Ishita complained of a pimple on her cheek, four days before the farewell, Pallavi knew she had found the *Achilles' heel* in her first competitor.

"Ishi darling, this pimple … it's not only a mere pimple."

"Then what is it?" Ishita was never so serious.

"This is a blot on your thus far beautiful and sexy image. You are our pride for you are the only one who rules as far as boys' fantasies are concerned. And everyone knows you are the Miss Agnes School of our batch but …" The pause was deliberate.

"But what? Come out with it, please!"

"This pimple! It will surely ruin all the years of hard work for you. Your image will change. Someone else will take your place in the heart of all the aspiring Romeos. And believe me once something like that happens – even once – you won't be able to rule ever again. I am sorry for being blunt but what else friends are for if not telling the truth, right?"

Ishita nodded gloomily and looked at her pimple on the mirror. "What should I do then?"

"Skip the farewell." Prompt came the solution.

"What? Are you crazy?"

"I only care for you. These farewells, they come and go but an image that you are the most beautiful girl of our batch should be eternal, don't you think so?"

Ishita thought for a while and then nodded positive.

"But of course the final decision is yours. Whether you want to go to the farewell and let people remember you as the pimple girl or skip so that they miss you, alright, but remember you as the girl who would have been Miss Agnes had she been present in the farewell. It's your take really!"

Ishita started crying and subsequently went into depression. *One down*, Pallavi was happy.

The second girl was Rupali who herself played into Pallavi's hands.

"Hey what happened to your neck?" The girls were coming out of a movie theatre. Rupali looked at her friend, rather amused, and walked ahead. Pallavi soon caught up with her, leaving the others behind.

"Is that a love bite?"

Rupali blushed.

"Heaven shit! Who is the lucky guy?"

"Anil."

"Anil Sahu of Commerce?"

"Ya!"

"When did this happen?"

"Yesterday, at his place. His mom had gone to the market and we were left alone. He only wanted to kiss me at first. Then he wanted me to strip and once I did that the rest just followed."

"Wow! So you are the experienced one now!"

"Ya!" Pride was evident as smile on Rupali's face.

"Does your dad know?"

Rupali suddenly turned serious. "Hell, no!"

"And what if he does?"

"Hell! I guess."

"You have to do me a favour Rupsi baby."

"What?"

"Skip the farewell and I'll do you a favour too."

"What favour?"

"I won't tell your dad about this."

"Are you trying to blackmail me?"

"No. You were trying to cheat us all so kind of getting square."

"Cheat?" Rupali felt jittery.

"Look, sex helps the glow on our face. And that way you'll obviously look better than us, won't you? And what if you win the Miss Agnes School title? No one will ever know about the real reason behind your glow. Isn't that cheating? Won't that make you feel guilty? Tell me Rupsi would you be able to handle this guilt for the rest of your life? You see, guilt is a strange thing. It can drive anyone crazy. So I would recommend-"

"I won't attend the farewell." Rupali started sobbing; a little for what Pallavi told her and a lot for what she now thought could have been avoided at Anil's place. "I am feeling ashamed now. I shouldn't have done that."

"Don't worry everything will be alright." Pallavi provided her shoulder to her and caressed her hair and forehead. *Two down,* Pallavi was jubilant. *Only Shabnam is left.*

"Hey Pallo your skin is glowing babes." They met in a departmental store, "Which parlour did you go to?" Pallavi and Shabnam not only studied in the same school but also lived in the same neighbourhood. And were each other's favourite allergen.

"My mom did it for me."

"She did everything for you?"

"Ya!"

You low breed bitch! Shabnam was determined to dig out the truth.

"Hello aunty Shabnam here."

"Hello Shabnam. Pallo is not at home."

"Oh! Could you tell me which parlour she got her threading etc done from?"

"She did?"

Damn she was lying! "Ya actually our farewell is coming up so…"

"Well I got no clues beta. I'll ask her to give you a call when she comes back."

"No no aunty. In fact you just ask her the name I'll take it from you. No need to tell her about it."

"Okay, as you say."

It was the first thing Mrs. Vimani asked her daughter once she was home. "Pallo did you go to a parlour? That too without my permission!"

I only went to Shobha aunty. "To Maiden's."

"You went there? That's pathetic!"

"I am sorry I won't go there again."

"You'd better not."

In the evening Shabnam called up again.

"Hello aunty did you get the name of the parlour?"

"She went to Maiden's."

"Thank you."

"But listen, you don't-"

The line was already cut. And the night before the farewell Shabnam realized her blunder. The threading process didn't go well and most parts of her face were swollen. Her dreams of any title, of course, were shattered. *She'll pay for it one day;* Shabnam, while sobbing the entire night, kept telling herself.

"And above all I owe this to my friends." Miss Agnes School, Pallavi Vimani, ended her winning speech, at the lavish farewell party organized at the school auditorium, to a thunderous applause.

It was one of the happiest nights in Pallavi's life. The teachers, the staff, boys and even some of the girls were mesmerized by her looks. But amidst the ear-deafening music, party buzz and all the hullabaloo she did think about Dino once and suddenly felt restless from within. Whenever his thought blocked the light of her smile a shadow fell on her soul whose darkness was so consuming that it made Pallavi's core suffocate and suffer ineffably. Every time she wanted to forget Dino she failed miserably. It seemed impossible to substitute someone. The fact that she couldn't win Dino tormented her heart and probed her ego constantly. Victory, which was a way of life for Pallavi, suddenly – to her gross frustration – seemed out of reach as far as love was concerned. And in the end the escapist inside her created an alien identity, for herself more than for others, contrary to the real Pallavi who – buried inside her heart – was neither aggressive nor arrogant. The alien Pallavi, on the other hand, wore her attitude on her sleeves. The alien one wanted to shut out her pains whereas the real Pallavi was a simple child who desired an emotional pillow to rest all her unexplained heartaches.

It was funny. When she used to pass her nights thinking about Dino she never dared to think what life would be like without his presence but from the day she knew he was someone else's Pallavi churned up excuses for herself: *it was only a crush…it happens with everyone…we shouldn't take love seriously…I have other duties too…it's his loss not mine…whatever happens, happens for good*. And behind all those excuses was one solid reason: she wanted to sever herself from someone with whom she would have lived forever had her story been punctuated a little differently. *Only a little…* sometimes that's what makes the whole fucking difference, she concluded.

Love is the process of adhering individuals with the glue of indomitable feelings. It makes one a part of the other. But when someone – incorrigibly in love – wants to deliberately get away from her love isn't that, in a way, getting away from oneself? The answer always defeated her.

"What about you?" They had to shake her.

"Huh?" It was time for the real Pallavi to go.

"Which college will you try for?"

"Umm" the alien Pallavi took over again, "Whichever has had enough of good luck!" Her smile unveiled a naughtiness which was typical of her.

HAASIL

Weird, Nitin thought. I'll be narrating to him moments which were once his reason of being.

"By the way, where are my parents?" Haasil asked.

"Your father died when you were twenty and last year you lost your mother too. You have no siblings."

"The framed photo in the hall…"

"Ya, it's them."

"What about your parents?"

"They are in London with my sister. I have an elder sister, Bani, married with two kids. They'll be here during winter."

"And what about Palki's parents?"

"They are here in Mumbai."

"Why didn't they care to come and meet me?"

"They were there in the hospital when you were unconscious. After you were brought home they kept checking your status with me."

"But they don't want to talk to me directly."

"They want to but I have told them you aren't ready. I hope you-"

"Ya, I understand." Haasil's wandering eyes suddenly fell on his friend's ring.

"Are you married?"

"You see." Nitin's face read amusement, "Before marriage you believe in miracles and afterwards you *want* to believe in miracles...real badly!" They laughed. "I still believe in miracles." Nitin completed.

"What's her name?"

"Sanjana Mirchandani. We got engaged three months back."

"Congrats."

"Thanks." A few seconds passed by with no further query. Nitin hated people who hid themselves behind the sublime curtain of silence. But now, to his utter sense of self-disgust, he too was trying the same.

"So?"

Nitin looked at Haasil and realized he was waiting for him to begin.

"Alright." Nitin cleared his throat slightly. "Palki and you met for the first time in a train. The Kathgodam Express."

"Were you with me?"

"No. Most of what I'll tell you doesn't feature me. We were, as they say, Frenchie-friends and shared everything with each other."

"I get it. Carry on please."

"Fifteen years ago, on the twenty-fifth of December, your family had planned a trip to Nainital. Actually you, along with your parents, had gone to your father's friend in Kolkata. The trip was planned ad hoc from there. Palki, with her parents, was also there in the same train but it was only in Lucknow you saw and met her for the first time.

It was six in the morning and when the train stopped at the Lucknow station for about twenty minutes, you went out for a stroll. Your parents – since you didn't tell them you were getting down – were worried and started a frantic search for you. It was near a book stall where Palki found you before others. She later admitted watching you since the journey began."

"What exactly did she ask me?"

"She asked you your name and told you about your parents' concern."

"What was she wearing?"

"You never told me that."

There was a pause after which Nitin continued, "Anyways, you guys talked all the way to Haldwani. Though both your families took different cars from there to Nainital but not before you guys exchanged your addresses. She used to live in Kolkata then. You guys kept in touch through letters for a year after which her father was transferred to Delhi. She joined our school in class seven."

"We were in Delhi?"

"Yes. Work brought us to Mumbai. My ancestral house is still there in Pahar Ganj."

"And mine?"

"You are actually from Mumbai. Since your dad worked in Delhi so most part of your childhood passed there. After his demise, of course, your mother shifted back."

Nitin, tickled by nostalgia, smiled. "In school the boys were jealous of you for Palki was beautiful in a dream-like way and the girls were jealous of her for you were the most handsome among us. To tell you the truth even I was a little jealous looking at both of you because you looked so perfect together. I always believed in the magic of love but Palki and you showed it to me. You know what I mean. Thus, the initial jealousy turned into admiration and finally to happiness for it was great to see the idea of perfect things wasn't just a fallacy. May be its uncommon – true love – and may be it happens only to some rare species of lucky people but it does happen.

When Palki joined us it was not like an initiation of something new but seemed more like the continuation of an old friendship. I remember Palki, each year, used to tie me a *Rakhi* but surprisingly you never qualified for it. The dumb ass that I was then I never could guess the obvious.

It was in class eight that you guys proposed to each other. That too together! The day she had kept a note in your diary you'd asked me to tell her about your feelings." They shared an overt smile.

"From time to time the boys used to complain about you for you were the one whom everyone fancied. Some of them even tried to gang up against you. Of course they could never go past me. And the girls! Gosh! They used to cry their heart out in front of me for you were committed. I remember once a girl told me you were the first love of at least seven girls of our batch! Crushes happen but first love?"

Haasil tried to look humble.

"After class ten we both took science. You were the topper then but in class twelve we both topped. Oh yes! There is one important thing that happened in class eleven. You experienced your first kiss with Palki. I wasn't there but I was after your life till you narrated me the entire episode.

Those days you used to pick her up from her English tuition class on your way from Physics tuition class. Sorry I forgot to mention she chose Arts after high school. Anyways that day it was raining and just like they show in films you had only one umbrella between the two of you. I thought, and knew, you had planned it that way but you never confessed doing it. Forget it. You two were on your way home when you intentionally parked your bike beside the road. You always liked getting drenched in the rain. I remember you used to say rain is nature's emotions. Seeing you getting wet in the rain Palki too joined and then it happened...your first kiss in the rain."

Haasil thought about the bizarre vision of seeing the couple kiss.

"We went to IIT Roorkie together whereas Palki continued with Arts in Delhi itself. After graduation we went for our MBA. You got into IIM Ahmedabad and I went to Wharton Business School. A year after our entrepreneurial endeavor – NH Consultants – was formed Palki and you got married."

"Where did we go for honeymoon?"

"Before that there is something interesting I want to tell you. It was Palki's idea to get married in two more ways apart from the obvious Hindu style. You two experienced a *Nikah* as well as a Church marriage. For Palki love was secular and so was your marriage. You know what? She was a woman for whom any man would readily smile through – let's say – the unhygienic parts of life."

"Did you say was?"

"Oh! I am sorry. She is still that way of course." *Don't repeat that,* Nitin rebuked himself and carried on. "For honeymoon you wanted to take her to Venice but it was her idea to go to not one place but the whole of India."

Nitin wetted his lips and observed Haasil's blank stare at the ceiling. There was a sudden frown on his face and he turned towards Nitin.

"Do you honestly think I'll be my real self again? Ever?"

"Oh yes!" *Till you remain far from the truth…* "You definitely will be your real self soon."

"Hmm. Now that I know something about her and us, as well, I want to talk to Palki."

"Sure."

"When?"

"Today will be tough. Lets see-"

"Tomorrow." Haasil was conclusive.

"Tomorrow." Nitin swallowed a lump.

Few minutes later Nitin took his leave perspiring profusely. He was in his car when he got a call from Palki's father.

"*Namaste* uncle."

"*Namaste* beta. How is Haasil?"

"Progressing but slowly."

"Okay."

"Any news of Palki's body?"

"No. The police is still on with the search but nothing positive has happened so far. I guess we'll have to accept the obvious." His voice was brittle.

"Let the authority do their job. You don't worry, okay?"

"Yes. At least Haasil is alive." Palki's father choked.

"The engine of my existence was chugging along, alone, on the track of life. Then you happened and the bogies of happiness, alacrity, purpose, zeal, ambition and reason – all, joined on."

Haasil felt a hand nudging his shoulder gently. *Palki is here!* A voice within him cried out. He opened his eyes to see Jennifer.

"Dinner is here." She said and brought the food trolley near the bed.

Haasil, sitting up on his bed to have dinner, paused momentarily to look at Jennifer.

"Have you ever been in love?"

The violent love-making extravaganza that took place each weekend when she met her husband suddenly flashed in front of Jennifer's eyes.

"Yes. I love my husband."

Haasil smiled in appreciation. "Love is beautiful, isn't?"

"Oh, yes! It's the creator's only masterpiece."

"And marriage?"

Something crossed Jennifer's mind bringing forth a silly smile on her face. "Jacob, my husband, often tells me how the idea of getting married used to give him the creeps. He loved his bachelor days and no way was ready to retire from it. Flirting around, bird watching and whatever it is that hallmarks bachelorhood was what he enjoyed the most and any kind of commitment was alarm bells. Then he met me and since then he only conforms to one thing: marriage probably is the only humane institute designed by human. True love, I tell you, is always a life-altering experience. Or may be it's the experience that actually helps one synchronize with life. "

"You said you love your husband…"

Pride rejoiced in Jennifer's eyes.

"…So tell me, will you ever be able to forget him…by any means?"

"No." It was a quick, sharp and a crisp reply. "Love", she sighed before continuing, "Happens once – you get it or you lose it but be rest assured, you never come out of it."

"True enough." It was a murmur.

The silence in the room allowed the two to be lost, for a while, within the kaleidoscope of their personal thoughts. Haasil turned slightly to his left and brought the photograph, from under his pillow, in front of him.

"This is Palki, my wife." He gave the photograph to Jennifer who stretched forward a little, perused the photo and handed it back to Haasil. "She is so beautiful."

A proud smile highlighted his face. "You mean my life is so beautiful."

"Ya!" She liked that, "Something about her face tells me she is a caring and understanding lady. Am I right?"

Haasil gave her a quick, serious glance and Jennifer instantly realized her mistake.

"I am sorry. I didn't mean it that way."

He turned his head towards the window. The rhythmic sound of the rain lashing the streets was subtly audible. *Sometimes the weather outside is the reflection of an inner build up.* He looked at the photograph again and unwillingly rubbed his eyes.

"You don't have to be sorry for it's not your fault. The first time I opened my eyes in the hospital I thought I was dead. I know its stupid – one can't think and be dead at the same time – but I really thought I was gone. Still, that was absorbable. Then – and I don't know why – a sense of loss flapped in my guts. A kind of loss that wouldn't have allowed my life to be *life* again: even if I continued to breathe, even if I cared to smile and even if I stubbornly held onto the belief that tomorrow shall be a diamond. For, every diamond of tomorrow, with the polish of today, becomes a useless stone. What does one do next…doesn't matter really for I knew I had lost something precious. And personal.

I opened my eyes and saw Nitin. I didn't recognize him at first but he told me he was my friend since kindergarten. The way he has, since, taken care of me only a genuine friend can do that. Isn't?"

Jennifer was listening intently and thus, when the question was shot, she didn't realize it was awaiting a response. Only after looking at Haasil's glance she surmised the obvious. "Ya…sure."

"But I didn't tell them – neither Nitin nor the doctor – one important thing. I initially thought it was happening because of the sedatives etc but after I saw this photograph…"

"What was happening?"

Haasil stopped caressing the photograph and looked straight at Jennifer. "A voice was constantly haunting me…I was arrested by it because it told me things which I felt I have heard somewhere but when and where? No idea."

"Next I had visions of a girl and a boy. Don't ask why I was experiencing them for I myself got no goddamn clue. The face was not clear till I saw her photo…my wife…Palki." There was a momentary silence and Haasil started again. "I can't wait to talk to her tomorrow. Nitin hasn't told her anything fearing her reaction. Thank God, for that means she loves me a lot." He smiled.

"If you don't mind could you please tell me more about your visions?"

Haasil's smiling face darkened and then, after a gap of a glance, it was a smiling dawn again. "Sure. At first the visions happened only in my dreams. I saw myself fighting a stormy night and the high waves of a sea to reach someone. I tried forgetting it but it kept boomeranging. As days passed I started having visions with open eyes as well. A girl and a boy, wearing a red tie, white shirt and black lowers, ambling together hand in hand – the same couple sitting across a table, probably dining, in a romantic ambience – few hillock of waves coming and wetting two pair of innocent legs – two heads, as silhouettes, one resting on the other's shoulder with a sudden glimpse of the sun between them – the girl comes running from somewhere and jumps onto the boy and they fall on the warm sand as a dying tide mingles with their youthful bodies – the girl, wearing a flowery white wedding gown, is standing with a bouquet of red rose, while the boy, dressed in a formal suit is all set to kiss his bride in front of a Church, a priest and probably a small gathering – they are in a car smiling and teasing each other and then...blank."

"Though I don't seem to remember anything of my past explicitly but this accident has helped me realize two significant things: firstly, if you really love someone nothing can come in between; neither any irony of life nor any tryst of destiny. And second, true love doesn't have a tense: it's never future, present or for that matter, past."

Moistening his lips slightly, Haasil preferred to talk. "I say I love my wife but I don't know how things will turn up considering my position. I know she is my wife, I know I love her and I also know she loves me but what I don't know are those small, subtle yet sublime details and secrets that epitomize a husband-wife relationship."

"But your wife remembers all that."

"That's the relief. But would she care to provide me the time I require and in a way, need?"

"You say she is your wife. Then why wouldn't she?"

"I hope" Haasil glanced at the ceiling, "And pray."

May love take the cake, Jennifer made her own silent prayer and got up. "You should sleep now."

Haasil obliged and moved slightly to straighten himself while Jennifer pulled the bed sheet till his chest. She drew the curtains and grasping the cordless phone walked out of the room. The first thing she did, after coming down to the hall, was connect to Nitin.

"Yes Jennifer, what's up?"

"Is Mr. Sinha supposed to talk to his wife tomorrow?"

The reply took some time to come.

"He told you about it?"

"Ya…in fact I think it'll definitely help him recuperate faster. From whatever he told me I think he loves her very much. And I believe same is true for her too."

"Of course. I'll surely get her on phone tomorrow. What is he doing now?"

"He has just gone to sleep."

"Good. Take care of him. You have been a blessing."

"Only doing my duty."

The phone call ended and Nitin, before continuing with his business meeting, thought, *I'll surely get Palki on phone for him tomorrow…I surely will…if someone, from somewhere, tells me how to connect to the dead…*

SWADHA

When Patel *Bhai* offered her exactly the kind of flat she was looking for in the posh locality of Vashi, Mumbai, at fourteen thousand a month rent Swadha didn't care to think about the cons of it, if there was any.

The flat was on the eighth floor – the topmost – of the apartment which not only kept her away from the rest but also gave her that much necessary proximity for a tête-à-tête with the sky, the stars and the moon whenever her nights were quiet with the mood of loneliness.

Sitting indolently, because tomorrow's name was Sunday, with one of the instrumental version of Stevie Wonder song playing in the bedroom, serenading her emotional weather, Swadha was carelessly sipping chilled Coke from a can. Its sudden salty taste brought her back to the realm of reality. She rubbed her eyes and sipped from the can again. *I hope he is doing fine*, Swadha thought. She wanted to see Haasil – at least once – but was not allowed. In fact nobody was. The accident was gruesome – she was told – and his wife was presumed dead. *Is that good news?* Swadha was ashamed of even thinking that way. But given the gravity of any situation profit is the first tide to hit the shore of a human mind. *Haasil is single now and I love him. I always will. Earlier I had reserved my feelings for him but now should I* ... something happens to someone in present because something is impending on someone else in future.

Few bubbles, floating in the air, called for her attention. *Am I dreaming?* Swadha peeped out of the large window frame and saw the little girl of her neighbour blowing soap bubbles into the dark sky. As the bubbles, pushed by air, flew across her Swadha busted them, one by one, with gentle exhalation. *Oh!* How pathetically she wished the issues of life to be soap bubbles. She could have busted them anytime to her liking and they would have vanished. *Gone!* But that's not to be. No matter how much one craves to move on few things always stick on to one's existence.

For example the past.

With the means of money – an antidote to law – Mr. and Mrs. Kashyap already knew they were going to have twins. Though the gender of every next-generation Kashyap had always been masculine – a mere coincidence misinterpreted by the Kashyap family as a divine influence on their pedigree – still celebrations didn't seem to cease.

A grand family get together was organized and there was festivity in everyone's mood. The Kashyaps, already a success in the field of ceiling fans and air coolers, announced a new business line – manufacturing of ball point pens – as a toast to the arrival of their seventh generation of business honchos.

The family astrologer helped decide the names of the new arrivals: Sourav and Gourav. But when the delivery happened and only one cry was heard, the Kashyap family – to their aghast, bewilderment and disgust – was forced to forget Gourav as one of the twins was born dead. God's irreparable blow to the Kashyap's much inflated ego and tradition came when they learnt that the other twin was of the weaker sex.

Sourav, in the *Naamkaran* ceremony six months later, became Swadha Kashyap.

The bad thing was Swadha had someone whom she called *papa* but she never got any father's love. The worse thing, though, was she didn't know why. She was, Swadha realized early, the only *beti* amidst the rest of the women in the family who were either a *bhabhi* or a *chachi* or *ma*.

"Who decides whether one will be a girl or a boy?" She once asked her mother. The only one, who, Swadha felt, actually cared and was aware of her existence.

"God." Her mother replied. She always feared the day when her daughter would realize her gender and also the *hidden costs* that came with it.

"My teacher says if we pray truly and regularly then our prayers get answered. Is that true?"

"Yes dear."

"If I pray with all my heart then will I be able to grow up into a boy?"

Her mother looked at her, caressed her cheeks, and said, "I too thought the same way when I was of your age Jilly." She kissed her forehead faking a smile. Swadha liked being called by her nickname. "But when I grew up I realized being a woman is always a better idea."

"You mean *papa* will love me even if I become a woman?"

"Yes."

"How soon will I become a woman?"

Sometimes it takes an era to become a woman and sometimes an instant, her mother thought. "You'll...soon."

Swadha attained puberty when she was ten. The steady growth of the chest made her believe that one day every other part of her body would also grow alike till she resembles a lady Hulk after which she would have to live alone in a far away land. *But then am I not all alone now too?*

Whenever she wanted to share her feelings, thoughts or any experience Swadha found her father and other members of the house either too busy with conversations on business or simply indifferent towards her pleas. *How come they have time for Bunty?*

One day Swadha secretly compared Bunty's and her report cards.

The marks were almost the same. But soon an inner voice made her discover one major difference. *Silly Jilly! Look at this*: his gender read 'M' and her 'F'.

Every year Swadha eagerly awaited her *papa's* approval to accompany the family on their annual visit to the *Vaishno Devi* Temple only to be left behind at home, in the end, with a maid servant and Mahesh, her youngest uncle.

At thirty, Mahesh was a frustrated toad. Since he had neither a leader's nor a student's instinct as far as business was concerned he was made to do all the errands of the house in exchange for a small room by the kitchen and a lifelong security for food and shelter. Twenty four-seven he reveled in booze and was obsessively compulsive regarding sex.

Once, when the family was away, Swadha, because her mother was not there and the maid was sleeping, preferred to complain about her acute menstrual pain to her uncle.

"What happened?" Mahesh, behind the garb of uncle's love, never missed a chance to play with her privates.

"I think I am bleeding."

"From where? Show me."

Though Swadha was caged with an overt shyness still she lowered her dress. *He is my uncle after all.* He immediately took her into his room and made her lie down on his bed.

"I have a medicine for you but you have to be quiet."

"Ok."

Mahesh brought a clean cloth rubbed it between her legs and once she was cleaner, slowly took out his penis.

"Where is the medicine?"

"Inside this." He held the semi-erect penis in his hand, "I will enter it in you, push it few times and then the syrup will be inside you."

Swadha didn't have a clue as to what he was saying. Or doing. She had had medicines earlier too but none of them were attached to anyone's body and more importantly nobody inserted them inside her vagina.

"Oh! It pains!"

Mahesh had only entered half. "Ssshhh." And he continued.

With the third push Swadha realized her uncle was doing the right thing for she had seen him doing the same with the maid too. *May be she also suffers from my kind of pain.*

As Mahesh seemed lost in the smoke of carnal pleasure he suddenly felt his back bone cracking. He pulled out his penis and screamed his vocal cord wide. He turned around to see the maid standing behind him with Bunty's cricket bat. As he stood up she hit him on his forehead. Mahesh fell on the floor, unconscious. Swadha was too dumbstruck to even cry. The maid quickly took her upstairs to her room and dialled Mrs. Kashyap's number.

It took the family two days to cut short the trip and return home. The moment Mr. Kashyap saw Swadha he leaped and hugged her as tightly as he could as if securing his most treasured prize from the werewolf world. For a moment Swadha thought it was, again, one of her reveries but when her *papa* looked at her with wet, guilty eyes she felt the pinch of reality. This was the moment she was waiting for since birth! Her prayers were answered at last!

A smile touched Mr. Kashyap's lips seeing his daughter's innocuously flummoxed face. He wanted to kiss her, cajole her, protect her and make her feel secured like a true father but there was something – with no concrete definition – that stopped him from doing so. And finally he chose not to fight it.

Life, thus, continued to be a kingdom of loneliness where Swadha was the king, the queen and also the subjects. Though she relentlessly tried to come out of that kingdom by befriending people she liked in school but soon she realized friendship was the most common disguise people adhere to in orde⁻ to satisfy a interest. Though she too longed for a boy friend like many of her classmates but was skeptic whether he too would neglect her eventually for being a girl. Precisely then she came across something which connected her to a certain Swadha that she never knew existed within her. Thy name was Orkut.

It was fun. Reading others interest, hobbies, activities, relationship status, testimonials, ideal match and the like. Even without meeting the person she got to know so much. Their scraps told her what they were going through in life. Her friends list started increasing sequaciously enough with most of them being boys. Swadha made two profiles: one was her true self and the other fake, in the name of Mahek. And scraps started pouring in.

Rohit: *can we be friends?*

Swadha: *Sure! What do you do?*

Mahek, after a week of exploration and cultivation by Swadha, stepped in.

Mahek: *Tell me do you lust for Swadha? I can hook you up with her.*

Rohit: I sure do.

Rejected! Swadha thought.

Raja: *Hi! Care for a genuine friendship?*

Swadha: *Why not?*

Mahek: *Hey Raja want to see Swadha's naked pics?*

Raja: *Like mad!*

Ignored!

First she befriended a guy and in case she felt anything for him, tested him being Mahek. This went on for more than a year by the end of which Swadha had rejected dot ninety eight proposals. Why do boys fake so much? Is sex the only reason why boys get attracted to girls and towards relationship in general? They will say 'I love you' and the first thing they do to prove it is ask you to open your top. Won't I ever meet a real man who would respect and love me; both the inner and the outer, me. Or, isn't there any real man? Swadha was about to give up when Rajesh happened. Again via Orkut.

Rajesh: *I liked your profile. Can we become friends?*

Swadha: *Ok!*

After a month…

Mahek: *You seem to like Swadha, is that right?*

Rajesh: *Yes but who are you?*

Mahek: *Well I have her naked pics…u want to check those up?*

Rajesh: *Just fuck off!*

Not bad!

Mahek: *I know you lust for her! Accept it.*

Rajesh: *I accept you are an ass.*

Not bad at all!

Mahek: *She is 32-28-30.*

Rajesh: *You sick-nymph shut the fuck up!*

Pass!

Rajesh: *Who is Mahek?*

Swadha: *A bitch!*

Rajesh: *Right, she keeps telling me disgusting things.*

Swadha: *I know. But she won't do that from now on.*

Rajesh: *Who is that guy in your friend list? Your boy friend?*

Swadha: *He is Bunty my cousin. I am very much single.*

Rajesh: *Good. Can we meet once? If it's not a problem with you.*

Oh! My first date! He is truly in love with me. Finally I have met the *real* man! He will meet me…propose me…I'll say yes…a beautiful relationship will start and then one day he'll again propose me … this time for marriage and few years down the line I'll proudly announce I am married to someone I know from my school days …how many can boast about that? Swadha was beaming.

Swadha: *Sure we can meet. My board exams are scheduled for next month. May be after that.*

Rajesh: *Sure thing.*

Phone numbers were exchanged. He found her voice sweet and she thought he sounded cute. And when Swadha's exams got over they chose Barista to meet up for the first time.

Rajesh was already waiting for her when she entered Barista at Hazrat Ganj, Lucknow. He was wearing a red skin hugging T-shirt with denim as lowers while she was wearing a white salwar-kameez along with her favourite white pearl ear rings and necklace as accessories. They had exchanged photographs long back so identification wasn't a bother.

"Hi!"

"Hi!" He stood up and pulled out a chair for her to sit, "Please." After that he sat down too.

Etiquette! "How are you?" She asked, finding it difficult to adjust to the sudden knot in her stomach and the fast beats her heart orchestrated. We all want our love story to be perfect from the word go whatever, though, is the eventuality, she wondered.

"What will you have?" He forwarded the menu to her. Swadha's nervousness was evident from the manner her both hands, holding the menu, shook. She didn't know what to say. All her favourite romantic movies showcased a particular fashion in which a cute love story began.

51

And if, Swadha thought, she didn't read his mind and surmise his choice she would ruin the cute beginning.

"Hot Choco-Latte."

"Hot? I think its summer outside!"

You spoilt it silly Jilly! "I mean I *won't* have the hot one."

"Then should I order two cold Choco-Lattes?"

"Ya. Sure."

After the order was placed Rajesh kept the menu aside and looked directly at Swadha. "So school life's getting over, right? What's up next?"

"Not sure yet." She tried to sound docile. Boys respect simple and innocent girls, her classmates had told her. "But may be I'll apply for commerce both in Lucknow and Delhi University"

"That's good."

Suddenly there was silence. It was necessary she thought because it's in the language of silence, sometimes, that one feels the vibe of love properly and vehemently.

"Actually I want some help from you."

He wants a yes from my side!

"And I" He suddenly grasped her hand, "want you to promise me you'll help me in this."

She felt a tickle between her legs. "Promise." Swadha somehow managed to speak.

"I am in love with-"

Oh! I know that Rajesh. I also love you but first you complete. She closed her eyes momentarily.

"Bunty."

Her smile, few seconds later, turned into a frown. She opened her eyes while Rajesh, oblivious to her emotional quandary, continued.

"From the first time I saw his picture in your profile I fell in love with him. If you have ever loved someone – I am sure you must have – you'll be able to understand what I am going through. Could you please get us introduced? I know I could have done it myself but then I wouldn't have stood out. A good reference always helps in these matters. You know what I mean?"

No, Swadha wasn't getting it because she wasn't hearing a word. From a girl, who was all eager to experience her first date, she had suddenly turned into an android. Her senses cease to work. She sat there for few more minutes after which she excused herself.

Swadha came back home, switched on the computer, logged onto Orkut, clicked on settings and then on 'delete my account'. Next, without caring to shut down the computer, went to bed. Closing her eyes she knew it was only a matter of time before she wakes up again to realize Rajesh was still waiting for her at Barista. And that they had not met yet.

Alas!

HAASIL

What will you do if I die one day? Asked the girl.

I'll give you company and die too. Replied the boy.

No! The girl placed her palm on his mouth. *I was only kidding. If your life remains incomplete…so will be my death.*

From the time Haasil woke up he had only one thing in mind: *I'll talk to her today!*

As per the doctor's advice he had started to stroll in his house though under the strict supervision of Jennifer. Earlier he felt as if each and every muscle of his body has been shot at but slowly it was getting better.

Fresh from his noon nap, Haasil sat up on his bed and pressed the bell. Half a minute later Jennifer was in the room.

"Good evening. I'll get you the milkshake."

"Before that could you please open that wardrobe for me?" He pointed towards the same wardrobe, by the window side, from where he had got Palki's picture. Jennifer opened it and looked at Haasil for further instructions.

"What do you see?"

Jennifer frowned slightly and observed. "A few gowns, saris, couple of albums and few perfume bottles."

"Bring one gown, both the albums and one perfume bottle."

She did.

"Thank you." It was evident from the way he said the last two words that he wanted to be alone. Jennifer granted him the tacit wish.

Haasil sniffed the maw of the perfume bottle and then looked at its label: Marc Jacobs. This time he inhaled the fragrance deep within him and found himself reveling in the surreal presence of someone's words.

You know why I use perfume? Just to suppress my real odor…the one that was formed when our senses rubbed for the first time…I don't want to share it with anybody … not even you…

He kept the perfume bottle aside and caressed the gown. He brought it closer to his face and then covered his face with it. *Oh! I miss you*

Palki. Tears were on the verge of attaining freedom from the fortress of his eyes but he controlled himself. *Not now!* The gown was kissed softly and subsequently kept aside. Next, he opened one of the albums. In the first photograph he saw Palki and himself – all dressed in woollens –with a chain of snow capped mountains in the background.

How do we know who loves the other more?

The one who dies first does.

Why so?

The one who is left alive still has a chance to prove his love!

In the second photograph both of them were on a *Shikara* floating on the serene Dal Lake. A few photographs later they were standing infront of the Lotus Temple. The date and time were printed on the photograph itself while the location was written in fountain pen behind each. Another flip brought the Taj Mahal followed by the Lover's Point atop Jakho Hills in Simla, inside the Mayur Mahal suite of Taj Lake Palace in Udaipur, at the Wagha Border, Palki peeping out from a Kolkata tram, Haasil on a pony near Victoria Memorial and there were many more. Haasil picked up the other album. *Their marriage album.* A faint smile, exuding gratitude towards life, edited his face.

"Here, your milkshake." Jennifer gave the glass to Haasil who, with the album open on his lap, took it readily.

"You want to take the medicine now or-"

"Now."

Jennifer quickly pressed the leaflet allowing one tablet to pop out on her hand. As soon as Haasil swallowed it with the first gulp of the milkshake he spoke up, "You know what I feel seeing these pictures?"

"What?"

"Love is, truly, the weather of life."

"And tonight will be spring!" Jennifer said with amusement smeared on her face.

Haasil glanced at her once and a second later, blushed.

"What is the one thing you are dying to tell her on phone tonight?"

"I love you."

Jennifer almost had wet eyes. *God bless!* She quipped to herself. "Call me when you finish the shake." She was gone.

Lying straight, for almost an hour, Haasil kept perusing the faded memories captured on the photographs. And with each flip his urge to meet Palki, talk to her, listen to her and also make love to her steeped. The walls of his heart, like the stomach does when it's hungry for food, were starving for her nutritious presence. Though he was recuperating well enough still, there was a constant phantasmal feeling that some personal parts – for which he cared the most – had been amputated. As if the accident had turned him into Winter and he would be Summer again only following the Spring of her arrival. *How should I start?* Hi, how are you? Hi, I missed you. Hi, I love you! None of the three seemed right and he got piqued thus.

Haasil was about to close the album when he saw Jennifer entering the room urgently.

"Your friend is on the line." She gave the cordless phone to him

"Nitin?"

"Ya how are you doing?"

"Fine. You were supposed to call at ten tonight."

"I am sorry *dost* but I need to fly to Delhi tonight to clinch a business deal. I'll be back by the day after."

"That's alright."

"And so I'll connect you to Palki the day I return."

The reaction came after a momentary hiatus.

"What's your trip has got to do with Palki calling me up?"

Careful, Nitin reminded himself. "Nothing. Absolutely nothing!"

"Then why not tonight?" A nervous pause again. "You sure before the accident we connected well? Be honest Nitin, I won't mind."

"Oh! Please don't think that ways."

"Then why do you always behave suspiciously when I talk of Palki? We have been out of touch since my accident and being my wife she didn't care to get in touch even once? Come on what is it Nitin, tell me."

"As I said there's nothing." It was difficult for him to lie but he somehow held on. "Actually she still thinks that you haven't returned to Mumbai. I lied to her about the unavailability of your mobile's network too. Now she is awaiting your return."

"Why don't you simply tell her that I have returned?"

"What if you don't sound normal to her? It might result in unnecessary anxiety. Please be patient for some more time."

"You sure she loves me, right?"

"She loves you as a woman should or can love a man. No doubt on that."

"Okay." After few rapid breaths, "I'll wait."

"Thanks. I'll be gone now and will call you next from Delhi. Take care, bye."

Nitin ended the call, finished the drink in a trice and staring at the empty glass ordered the bar tender, "One more please. Make it stronger."

Haasil gave the phone to Jennifer and as she left the room he straightened himself on the bed once again and rested the album on his chest. Slowly, he closed his eyes thinking about Palki. Sometime later, when sleep caught up with him, a world opened with a welcome message…

You are the minute hand and I am the hour hand. The female said and continued,

"You move that's why I move."

"And what about the second hand?" The man queried.

"That's our love for each other. We move because, and only if, it moves."

PALLAVI

The first thing Pallavi did on the day of joining V.J Bhavna College of Arts was check out the mark sheets of the second and third year students pinned on the notice board adjacent to the administration office.

"Do you have any friend or acquaintances here?" It was one of her batch mates.

"Not really but some of the names will help me out."

At the end of the third day as the students were getting out of the class a bunch of guys came in, shut the door behind and asked every one to take their seats.

"All the Senor and Senorita, we are your seniors." Said one. "That only means we own your ass for the next one hour!" Said another.

They made one guy stand up on a desk and ordered him to do

hundred sit ups. One of the seniors came and sat in front of Pallavi, took out a cigarette, lit it, puffed once and blew the smoke on her face. "You look like an actress. What's your name?"

"Shweta." She lied.

"Nice name. Are you a virgin?"

Vikram Goel – that's what the girl called the meaty dude at the canteen. Could he be the same one whose name I saw at the bottom of the third year students? Usually the brawn ones rank last. Umm…Let's try.

Pallavi looked straight into his eyes and said, "No, I am Vikram Goel's girl friend."

The name took a moment to sink in and when it did the boy choked on the cigarette smoke. *On target!* With a sudden surge of politeness the guy asked her to leave the room.

Whenever a chance conjured up Pallavi either stuck onto Vikram Goel's gang inside the campus or hovered around his bike, during free time, as if waiting for him. The camouflage was of such superlative order that everyone, and at times Vikram Goel himself, thought she was a part of them. Meanwhile the ragging session went on for another couple of weeks and each time, before the ordeal, Pallavi was gracefully escorted out of the classroom.

"Fate fears the Pallavies and fucks the babies!" She explained it to her friends who were stupefied by her guts.

During the welcome ceremony of the juniors she was compelled to come out with the truth in front of the seniors and super-seniors. Some applauded her grey cells while many took it as an insult. Thus, punishment it was, at last, for Pallavi. She was asked to pay all her senior's booze bill. *That's no punishment … that's a chance for me to show I have already got what others become a dog for…money!* Pallavi told herself and, almost boisterously, sponsored the grand booze party.

Within the first six months of college Pallavi became the talking-encyclopedia for all the college romances. Who is fucking whom, who is time passing with whom and who is bitching about whom and why, which guy is single and who all are ready to mingle – Pallavi, as if, was doing Honors at it.

"Is Akshit trying to woo Sonam?"

"No. It's her sister he is after."

"Hey do you know Sunita is not a virgin?" Sonali thought she could topple Pallavi on this.

"But do you know she only did it in the missionary position?" Pallavi shut her up.

"You think you know everything?" Sonali was sarcastic.

"Get your facts right darling. I not only know everything ... I can do everything too."

"Oh! Really?"

"Are you challenging me?"

"What if I am?"

"Okay! So what do you want me to do?"

Sonali thought for a while. "The entire college knows that Varun and Shefali are committed like mad."

"Ya, so?"

"Break them up!"

"And what do I get as a prize?"

"Whatever you say!"

"I'll date your boy friend for a day."

That was when Sonali realized her mistake but by then it was late. Too late, Pallavi thought and smiled at her.

The next morning, as soon as Pallavi entered the college campus, it was preying time for her. She was awake the whole night devising a plan to win. And by dawn she did hatch one.

Shefali was going towards her class room when Pallavi interrupted her.

"Hey Shefali sweetie, where have you been these days? Saw so less of you! Everything's fine?"

"Ya. All's well. But right now getting late for the class."

"Is it that important?"

"I guess so. I'll join you at the canteen later." Shefali said and walked inside the class room.

"Okay!" Pallavi went to attend her own class in the canteen where her students, the ones who hailed her guts, were waiting for her.

After an hour she saw Shefali entering the canteen with Varun. Pallavi, with a hunter's instinct, ambled across to their table.

"Hey, what's up?"

Shefali and Varun quickly exchanged a not-again look and together turned towards Pallavi.

"Hi! Lunch is up."

"May I?" Pallavi asked pulling a chair in front of them and before Shefali could react she said, "Thank you." And sat down with them.

"So how's life?"

"Cool! Busy with exam preparations."

"Exams? When are they starting?"

"Next week."

"Oh! Till they come within the twenty four bracket no tensions!" Pallavi started to play *Tabla* on the table and hum a latest Bollywood number. And suddenly she spoke up aloud, "Hey I have been looking for this one!" Before Varun could surmise what she was talking about his mobile phone was in Pallavi's grasp.

"Nokia is always sexy! What's the price?"

"Fifteen-"

"Wait let me check its features."

And all Shefali and Varun did was share a there-she-goes-again glance. After five minutes of thorough perusal Pallavi handed over the mobile phone to Varun. My job's done, she thought.

"Alright I'll catch you guys later. Its interval now so I am going to class."

As Pallavi walked off Shefali quipped, "We have interval between classes she attends a class between intervals."

The Indian History professor was giving his lecture in a way that forced the students to wonder whether he was a part of that history too. And if no then why the heck not?

Pallavi was sitting beside Tania; few rows ahead of Varun and a row behind Shefali. As she saw Tania glancing at Varun, her secret crush, Pallavi stealthily took her cell and messaged Varun.

Hi! I love you!

The reply came instantly. *Hey jaan I love you too!*

Gosh, it's working! Pallavi thought. She had renamed Shefali as Tania and Tania as Shefali in Varun's cell in the canteen itself. Thus, her message to Varun from Tania's mobile phone read Shefali in his inbox.

Pallavi messaged again.

I am feeling very....today...

Feeling what???

To be alone with you...only you...and me...

Even I am feeling the same. Should we go to my place?

Umm...okay! Will we do the entire thing?

Well…we will go wid the flow…

Done! I'll be waiting for you after the class … in the canteen…

Can't really wait baby!!!

As soon as the class got over Pallavi, almost with the speed of a blink, did two things: messaged Sonali asking her to be present in the canteen and stopped Shefali by the classroom door.

"I wanted to show you something Shefali. But promise me you won't get upset with Varun." With her boy friend's name on Pallavi's lips Shefali instantly knew something was wrong.

"Talk to him because talking helps clear out things." Pallavi tried to sound innocent.

"What are you talking about?"

"I don't know whether I should show this to you or not but-"

"Oh cut the crap. What is it?"

"It's about Tania and Varun. Look at these smses."

For a moment Shefali didn't know what to do and then suddenly, snatching the cell from Pallavi, she stormed towards the canteen and what happened there only helped Pallavi date Sonali's boy friend the very next day. Though any explanation wasn't a part of the bet but Pallavi, since she knew about the ineffable pain a love wound generates within, was more than happy to confess everything in order to embolden the couple for a patch up.

That night when Pallavi went to bed she felt a strong urge to cry. And she did. There was something between Varun and Shefali which made her miss someone. Since the school farewell night she decided not to think about Dino but time and again she missed her first love. *Do I miss him because I never got him? Or, do I miss him because I know I'll never love anyone like him, ever?* Pallavi never got any answer. It's like the first time a man runs a razor on his cheeks. And come what may the skin never remains same. The skin of my life too hasn't been the same since I became aware of Dino's existence…since I fell in love with him. Her cries turned into sobs. Whose fault is it when someone doesn't understand your love for him? Who is to be blamed if you fall for someone who already is committed? What do you decide to do when, on one hand, you are insanely in love with someone and on the other you know he won't ever be yours? *Never ever!* Which medicine do I prescribe myself for a bleeding heart? Pallavi was biting her pillow hard to mute the sobs. At last, when her within was done with the emotional monsoon, Pallavi zeroed in on a solution. *The more I'll stay single the more he'll get a chance to torture me. I'll have to get a guy and probably fuck Dino out of my system.*

The search started inside her college and ended with a cousin's college senior. She saw him in her younger cousin's college fest album.

"Who is he?" Pallavi asked her cousin.

"Ronit Bhagat."

"Could you arrange a meeting with him?"

"What for *didi*? You like him?"

"Nay! Only a college project." She winked.

They met near one of the Café Coffee Day outlets in Connaught Place and after the initial introduction went inside together. They hit it well. Of course, Pallavi was the dominant and thus the steering of the relationship was in her hand.

They talked over the phone till dawn and dated after college hours. Ronit was intelligent, well mannered, decent looking, genuine at heart, was reasonably full pocketed every time and above all had no attitude. *I never wanted my guy to have what I already possess*, Pallavi was delighted.

There was one problem though. Ronit never took the first step. Once they were in Waves Cinema watching an English film play to a silent audience. Sitting on the last row with nobody on either side Pallavi knew it was the exact moment when she wanted her first kiss to happen. She slowly moved her hand towards Ronit and suddenly grabbed his arm. He looked at her only to find she was already looking at him. Pallavi, with eyes closed, leaned forward, with her tongue in a ready-steady mode. She parted her lips slightly expecting his in-between hers. She heard a whisper instead.

"Sorry dear, I don't have a condom."

Pallavi, in a flash, opened her eyes. She couldn't believe it. Her seductive look, that seemed once upon a time now, had transformed into a stern one.

"We don't need a condom to kiss, you dumb ass!" Pallavi walked off the hall fuming.

After several days of apologizing, and absorbing the humiliation of the phone being cut even before he could start, Ronit summoned all his dare and visited Pallavi's house carrying a bunch of red roses, few boxes of foreign chocolates, a four feet Archies sorry-card and stood in front of her with a face that exuded a genuine remorse. Still, Pallavi wasn't satisfied.

After the maid went away, leaving the two alone in the house, Pallavi took Ronit to her bedroom.

"I want you to strip."

Ronit, obediently, started stripping the chocolates off their wrappers.

"Uff!" Pallavi was riled. "Strip yourself idiot."

Ronit, with dropped jaws and frozen stature, gaped at Pallavi.

"Strip else I'll rape you." Pallavi quipped.

"But this isn't right. A girl can't rape a boy."

"Really?"

"Yes." Ronit was already swallowing lump after lumps.

"It's not about gender kido! It's about dominance! Now will you do it yourself or should I…"

Ronit quickly doffed his shirt. And when he finally stripped down to his brief Pallavi came close to him, looked down and then up again.

"Where has all your blood gone?"

Ronit didn't get her.

"Can't you do anything yourself?" She was looking at his underwear which showed no obvious bulge.

"I don't see you that way." Ronit said meekly.

Oh God! What is he?

"I love you but I don't lust for you."

"I am happy that you love me but don't you watch movies? People who love each other also make love. Don't you want to do that to me?"

"I want to but not now. It's better to do it after marriage."

Pallavi suddenly leaped forward and hugged Ronit tightly. Her breasts crushed against his chest and he was on the verge of surrendering to his hormones when he pushed Pallavi aside.

"If I love you and so do you then what's the harm if we wait till marriage? Don't you think being patient about sex is the ultimate test of commitment?"

Pallavi never saw Ronit again.

In the latter part of second year most of the students were actively pursuing part time jobs. It not only added to their resume but also gave them a sense of financial independence. Pallavi, at first, condemned it all as meaningless compared to the gossip sessions at the canteen and other on and off campus frolics. But from the time her own students started disappearing, one by one, from the campus after classes, Pallavi cared to enquire.

"What's up with Manvika, Sammy and Ranjana? Where do they vanish everyday?"

"Office." Vitika said.

"Office? What kind of office?"

"The kind where they pay if you work."

Pallavi pinched her hard to come out straight.

"Everyone's doing part time jobs dear. I thought you knew."

"I do. But I didn't know the fever has caught up with our group also."

"Well I too had an interview yesterday."

"Really? Where?"

"Zebra PR agency."

"And?"

"And I am joining them as a trainee content editor. They'll give me six thousand a month."

"Vitika" Pallavi came close to her. "Listen to me dear. Why are you doing this? For money?" Her friend nodded. "Do you seriously think people like you and me need to earn money? We should respect what God has given us. And He has given us our respective dads who are earning like anything, right?"

Vitika suddenly found herself listening intently. Only the other day she had fought with her dad over the job issue. But then she didn't think about what Pallavi was telling her now.

"Look *yaar*, chill *maar*. These part time jobs are for middle class losers. They need pocket money for they only got pockets but we got these." She showed their Gucci hand bags resting on the table beside them. "This is time for us to enjoy. *Masti-sasti* and all! You getting me? But if we waste this time burning our ass-fat for some company and that too for a shit thing like money then what'll be the difference between you, me and let's say Sunaina? We are the lucky ones and so it's our moral obligation to enjoy our luck. Tell me, have you ever wondered how our parents will react if they hear about this?"

Vitika, once again, thought about the duel with her dad.

"They'll assume their hard work for giving their children a happy life has gone to the gutters! Do you think they deserve that? Do you really think so?"

Vitika nodded negative and thanked Pallavi for enlightening her.

"So what will you do now?"

"Simple! I won't join them." They smiled and went to attend the last class for the day.

In the evening, Pallavi, after referring to the yellow pages, made an important call.

"Hello. Zebra PR agency?"

"Yes. How may I help you?"

"I want to apply for the post of trainee content editor."

"I am sorry ma'am that position has been recently filled."

"But she won't be joining for she has taken ill."

The reply came after some hush sounds.

"We'll wait for a week and then you can join us."

Pallavi punched the air, smiling.

"In case you pass the interview, that is."

"Sure."

The line went dead and Pallavi told herself, *Pallavi fails…only if she wants to.*

With time she started enjoying her office more than the job itself. The little flirt sessions with colleagues and sometimes seniors, the subtle sexual innuendoes shared with her clients and the passionate glances she threw whose sole purpose was to put men's right hand at work during nights: she reveled in it all! And when Sameer, head of corporate relations at Zebra PR and a compulsive womaniser, asked her out for a date Pallavi knew it was time to shed off an important tissue.

They went to the La Piazza at Hyatt Regency, gobbled some Italian dishes rich with exotic aphrodisiacs and immediately after they finished Sameer proposed the obvious. "At your place or mine?"

As the door to Sameer's two bed room flat at Dwarka opened the two stumbled in with their respective tongues licking the other's face ferociously. Benjo, Sameer's lapdog, came running to him but backed up. He knew his master didn't like interference when he was at work. And the work, a little unlikely, went till the wee hours of the night. The friction between a virgin vagina and virile vigor produced such fire on bed that it could easily put two flint stones to shame.

When Pallavi went home, the next morning, she headed straight for her room after convincing her mom it was only a late night study session at a friend's place. She slept like a politician till late afternoon and while taking a shower in the evening thought, "Yesterday I was a virgin. Today I am not. Has anything changed?" She observed her body. "Not really! Then why is sex such a taboo? Losing virginity early is no big deal!"

Third year of college saw Pallavi change seven boy friends after thoroughly *studying late nights* with each one of them.

And as her college life also got over Pallavi realized the fun, after all, had just begun.

SWADHA

"Are girls sinners?"

Her mother was a little taken aback with the query. As far as she knew her husband had changed his attitude towards his daughter and this question shouldn't have been asked. *Not now at least!* "Why do you ask darling?"

"Bunty told me all sinners are born as women in their next life. Is that true?"

"That's completely rubbish!"

"Then why is it that every month we bleed and suffer pain without any fault of ours? Or, are we at fault?"

"Even boys go through it."

"Don't tell me! I have never seen Bunty using a Whisper pad."

"What I meant was boys too undergo growth. And that's what you are also going through. It's normal."

"But why for a girl, to become a woman, normalcy means going through pain? A boy turns a man simply with age? Why is this bane designed only for us?"

"You see, no bane no gain. You should consider yourself lucky for you are a girl."

"No bane, no gain." *Point taken!* "But what gain?"

"You and your questions!" Her mother rubbed her nose against hers. "You'll realize the gains yourself, later." Her mother was thankful for her daughter, at seventeen, was still as innocent as before. It was a rarity. Children gain maturity so fast these days that their days of simple yet memorable joys get shortened in the process.

Immediately after Swadha's board results were out a surge of application processes began. A high percentage made her eligible for the best colleges in the country but ultimately – thanks to her father primal possessive attitude – only those applications which were aimed at the girl's college were posted.

"But why do you have to leave Lucknow? We have the best college for girls here. Why don't you simply go for IT College?"

"Daddy it's not only the college. I want to explore the outside world too. I'll learn more about life by staying away from all your protective endeavors. I am not saying I don't like it but I also want to see am I good enough to live independently or not. And mom only said where there's no bane there's no gain."

Finally parental emotions were taken care of and Swadha joined Saagar Vamshi College for Women in Pune. She enrolled for science and, again against her father's wish to buy her a small flat for her, put up at Eve House; the ladies hostel of the college.

After a month at Eve House her father's words made sense to her. The hostel girls were different. Some weirdly and the rest wickedly so. They discussed the private parts of boys. They watched porn sites in their lap tops. They smoked marijuana and the like. There were days when they forgot to dine or shower but never to drink. They fantasized, made dildos out of certain vegetables and some even told Swadha the various stimulating ways of female masturbation. During their ragging nights each girl was ordered to walk around naked in the room. Some were asked to moan squeezing their breasts and the others had to show the various sex positions on bed holding the poster of their favourite film actor. Their asses were slapped hard and few unlucky ones also had to enact vulgar role plays. Swadha abhorred all this. She didn't know what to do for co-operation was the only available option. Whenever she was alone, sometimes sobbing inside the toilet or awake with wide eyes on her bed past midnight or looking at her parents' photographs or sitting alone after a humiliating ragging ritual, her mother's words kept resounding in her conscious: no bane, no gain. And she stuck on.

After few months Swadha found herself adjusting surprisingly well with the surroundings. *Time...it even makes you adapt to total shit sometimes!*

Of whatever she heard, learnt or saw in the hostel or outside insulated her in some way. No longer was she shocked at anything. No longer was she unprepared for anything. Or so she thought. The most disgusting thing, Swadha learnt at Eve House, was, though, about herself. She realized there was an insatiable voyeur inside her. And to satisfy it she had to do things which otherwise, may be, she wouldn't have done.

Swadha used to pretend sleeping at nights whereas all her focus, invariably, used to be on what her room mate spoke on phone. And when her mate kissed on phone or made specific love sounds Swadha blushed to herself. At times she even checked her friend's undergarments in order to know who was secreting what and when. On weekends there used to be an assemblage of boys around the main gate of Eve House. They poured in with bikes and made noises with their flimsy horns misinterpreting it as music. And whenever any girl peeped out from the window they would sing some third grade item numbers to please them only to encourage a look of disgust. But no one complained for everyone, latently, liked it. After all, what sex is to man, praise is to woman. Some of the girls even sat down to decipher the probable meaning of the slangs and puns incorporated in the lyrics.

From time to time Swadha compulsively wanted to be in a relationship. Especially when her friends showed their Valentine Day's gifts to her or told her about the good times they spent with their boy friends or asked for one of her dresses to get ready for a date. After the Rajesh incident something inside Swadha told her she couldn't risk a disappointment again as far as love was concerned. She dreamed of someone – with a reasonably fair complexion, red thin lips, eyes that exuded as much eternal commitment as it did incorrigible naughtiness, smile that was cushioned with the kind of panache that ruins a woman of her calmness, charm that dwarfed life's problems, courtesy that would make her his die hard fan and demeanor that would convince her he was *the* man. But Swadha, to her dismay, was yet to meet anyone even remotely close. By the time she reached third year of college doubts, regarding the existence of her perfect man, outweighed the romance of it. And when Avantika, a good friend of hers, attempted suicide Swadha was convinced it was all a farce; love, commitment and the like.

Every girl in the hostel knew about Avantika's affair with Dhruv. But nobody bad mouthed it as they all knew how true their love was. The commitment was five years old, Avantika's parents also knew about Dhruv and the couple themselves were dead sure to get married once their professional life started moving. But right before their college farewell Avantika learnt Dhruv was double-timing her for the past couple of years.

"Don't worry Avni. Men are dogs." Rekha tried to console her friend.

"But dogs have breed." Swadha poured in.

Rekha gave her a stern look. "You said it! Dogs have breed. Men don't."

"But you said men are dogs."

"Oh shut up!" Rekha turned towards Avantika again. "Could you tell me exactly why you tried killing yourself?"

"I" Avantika choked and after a deep breath, continued. "I didn't know what to do. I loved him so much. Believe me I gave it all to the relationship and this is what he gave me. Tell me Rekha what else should I have done?"

"Did you kick his balls?"

"That would hurt!" Swadha shrieked.

"Really! Not more than a broken heart I guess. Listen Avni, I'll tell you why you should party for your break off." They looked at Rekha, flabbergasted.

"But first tell me why you think people have break offs?"

Both were blank.

"Almost ninety nine percent of relationships break because at least one of the two shows dishonesty – in whatever form or degree – towards it."

"What about the remaining one percent?" Swadha was inquisitive.

"I haven't thought about it. All I know is that relationship is like a baby and needs nurturing. The nurturing of trust, faith and honesty else it might turn spastic anytime. It needs a mother's milk of commitment as much as a father's secured presence. Didn't our parents skip their night sleep when we used to pee on our bed as kids? Likewise, a relationship also needs sacrifice on both sides. Didn't our dad adjust his most urgent office work when he heard we were suddenly taken ill? A relationship also needs that kind of timely adjustments. Though human beings – it's said – are blessed with emotions the irony is understanding someone else's emotions and acting in a way that it never gets hurt still remains an uphill task for us. Some try to give a damn about it and others, the assholes, they simply shrug off. And-"

Rekha wanted to continue but stopped seeing Avantika, once again, break into sobs.

"I…I gave him everything I had…"

"Did you guys fuck?"

Avantika broke further and hugged Rekha tightly.

"Don't worry Avni." Swadha spoke up, "If you gave your body so did he. It's not only your virginity at stake...it's the same for him as well...so calm down. It's not a big deal."

"You know what?" Rekha, while caressing Avantika's back who still was hugging her, looked at Swadha with intent, "If you are born without a dick then everything's a big deal. Don't you read newspapers? Teenage pregnancy is on the rise. And don't you question yourself about it? Everything is a man's responsibility but the moment a girl becomes pregnant it's her problem. Whenever any MMS or sex video hits the internet it's the girl's family who needs to hide in shame. If a girl is teased she needs to change her route to school, college or office. It's us who get doted non-stop by younger or older men traveling in trains, buses or auto rickshaws but it's us who suffer psychologically and feel frustrated and embarrassed about it. A man thinks taking a girl's virginity is the only way to rule and enslave her; morally, emotionally and of course physically. But does he ever – for a slightest shit of a second – think about our heart? We know the way to a man's heart is through his stomach and he knows the way to a pussy is by faking love or commitment. Basically men aren't men anymore."

"But there are girls too who ditch guys."

"Of course there are. Inside every woman hides a bitch and inside every man hides a bastard. Nobody can run away from it but if we talk numbers – thanks to India's irrational sex ratio – then you know the truth."

If that's the truth then won't I ever get anyone who would love me selflessly? Or, is selfless love too romantic a concept to happen in reality? After knowing all this shit that happens will I be able to give my cent percent to a relationship? Won't there be this constant sword of suspicion, from my side, hanging on any relationship I enter in future? Will the relationship, that way, ever be beautiful? Christ! That way can any relationship be beautiful? Swadha wetted her bone-dry lips.

"What should she do now?" She asked Rekha.

"Party to start with. If Dhruv was a good human being and loved you from his heart then he would have never done what he did. Not being in a relationship with you at least. And now he is no longer in your life. That means someone who never loved you has left your life. So don't you think that calls for a party?"

All the three girls kept looking at each other's face for sometime and then burst out laughing with Avantika somehow managing to smile stretching her tear soaked cheeks.

"After partying move on happily with life, learning from the mistake. And remember there are lots of people who still love you a lot darling." Rekha kissed Avantika on her cheeks.

"Thanks."

"From the next time onwards just think before you love anyone, okay?"

But can someone think and fall in love? Swadha slowly ambled out of the room following her friends.

Life after graduation began on top gear. More so because of a myriad of management admission tests that followed. Swadha secured ninety eight percent in the Common Admission Test and after a fiery round of group discussion and personal interview was selected at a premiere institute in Gurgaon for her post-graduate studies.

Power point presentations, case studies, lectures, campus activities, discussions, debates, projects, training, terminals: life became a schedule in the first year. And just when she thought she badly needed a break she met Soham at a inter college fest. He was pursuing MBA from an institute at Ghaziabad.

It was love at first sight for Soham and thus it was he who asked Swadha, though a tad apprehensively, her phone number. Even she was a little hesitant at first. *Silly Jilly! Are you running for the post of the next Mother Teresa?* Swadha eventually messaged him the number after a week long analysis. And they hit off well from the word hello!

Every time they talked over the phone one pleasant thing about the other was discovered. When their friendship aged by a fortnight Soham proposed through sms.

Mind if I say I love you?

Before he could anticipate anything the reply was there in his inbox.

Mind if I say me too!

Every Saturday Soham came to Gurgaon and they went for movies, ate out or sat inside his car parked by the Delhi-Gurgaon highway and chatted for hours. Within three months their reasonably chaste relationship graduated to that level where he started expressing his love physically to the discomfort of Swadha. Her experience had biased her against sexual expression of love. She confessed it soon to Soham.

"It's not sex dear." He told her. "We are only kissing and at most smooching and touching."

Isn't that the prelude? She thought but nodded in agreement.

On one of the Saturdays Soham invited Swadha to his place in Ghaziabad. *Silly Jilly! Its time to spread up! He'll fuck you properly after which you no longer would be of any interest to him!* But a no from her side would definitely strain the relationship, she wondered. She loved him and didn't want to disappoint him. Thus shutting the inner voice she decided to visit his place.

"Today will be the most important day of our relationship."

"I know." She sighed.

It was a rented house and there weren't any furniture except for three messy mattresses.

"Excuse these. I share the place with two more college mates. So-"

"I understand." She sat on the edge of one of the mattresses. He sat on another.

"Now listen to me carefully. I won't ask you anything but-"

Swadha couldn't hear the rest of it for she was in a world of her own. What needs to be done, needs to be done. She stood with eyes closed. *I know what you want*, she thought and started unbuttoning her shirt. After she doffed the shirt Swadha loosened the belt and stripped her jeans. Standing in her undergarments, for the first time in front of a guy, she tried hard not to think or feel anything. *Any moment now*, she thought, *he would come and stamp his print on me*. But instead of feeling a tempting touch she heard the noise of utensils. Swadha opened her eyes only to find the whole room consumed in darkness.

"What's up?" She asked confused.

"Shit!" Soham spoke from the kitchen. "I don't know where my friends have kept the candles. There's a power cut."

"Means?"

"Means there's a power cut. I told you to excuse me."

"You did?" She never heard it. "Of course you did!" Swadha hastily wore her clothes.

"Sorry I don't think there's any candle here."

"It's okay."

"Do you want to go out for a walk?"

"Not really."

"Then how can we talk…wait a second."

Soham sauntered to the small adjacent room and came back with a lighter.

"You smoke?" Swadha was surprised.

"Occasionally!" Soham lit a newspaper and now they could see each other better.

"Swadha" they were reading each other's eyes, "I really love you."

"I love you too Soham."

"But there is a problem dear. As you already know I lost my father during my adolescence and my mother is a heart patient. Last year she had undergone a by-pass surgery."

"Ya I know all that."

"She wants me to marry the girl of her choice."

For a moment Swadha didn't speak and then quipped a little loudly than necessary.

"But" she checked her voice, "Can't I be her choice? Am I not good enough?"

"You are just perfect. Believe me but she has already promised someone which I didn't know before I came in touch with you else I would have never dated you."

"But I love you."

"I too love you. A lot at that but I love my mom more than a lot. And I can't do anything without her blessings."

"Did you talk to her about me?"

"I did. But her health only worsened the next day."

Nothing was spoken for a long time after that. Words -- the most significant blessing for human – suddenly lost all its relevance. Swadha, impulsively, came closer to Soham and resting her head on his shoulder started crying. He too, she soon realized, was crying. This only stimulated her emotions and they together cried for the rest of the evening.

"I want you to know" Soham was choking, "I'll be always there for you."

A prolonged platonic hug happened between the two. They later realized it was the most romantic break-off they could have ever experienced.

Almost ninety nine percent of relationships break because at least one of the two shows dishonesty – in whatever form or degree – towards it.

What about the remaining one percent?

Swadha now knew about it. At least he would be my friend! But the next six months saw less and less calls from Soham's side. And whenever she called he was either busy with exams or simply didn't pick up her call. In the end Swadha accepted it. She was doomed to remain single forever.

"Firstly it's damn difficult to find true love and when you do find it – by chance or whatever – there's this pathetic piece of dogshit called destiny." Swadha told her room mate at the institute.

"I know but sometimes you simply can't do anything."

"Sometimes? Oh! Come on. Life doesn't deserve that modesty."

"But–"

"In fact I have already decided. From now on I'll only have my work and family as priorities. Nothing more and no one else. Why to run after something that's not made for me. When I came out of my home for the first time I had promised my parents and myself too that I wanted to earn my identity. This thing just happened. May be the break off was only a ploy to get me back on track for my goal."

"I agree with whatever you are saying but won't you ever get involved with a guy?"

"No." It was a straight answer.

"What about marriage?"

"Whoever my parents choose."

"And what if you don't fall in love with him?"

"Honestly, I don't give a damn anymore. Nothing on earth can alter my decision now."

Till the last phase of her post graduation Swadha did manage to hold onto her decision and focused all her pizzazz to academics. Before the final semester, with all the companies coming up, the campus started buzzing with pay package news, group discussions, mock interviews and candidate profiling. And when the first company – NH Consultant Pvt. Ltd – came every aspect of her decision went for a toss.

She was sure of all the homework regarding the interview. Twelve candidates were chosen from the group discussion round. Only eight were left after the HR round for the final selection interview.

Though her name was called out first, Swadha was still puffed with confidence. She opened the door slightly and peeped in to observe a big room with the interviewer sitting behind a relatively small aluminum desk. "May I, please, come in?" The silence made her stomach suffer a knot. And when he looked up at her, requesting her to step in, Swadha saw the face of the interviewer and recollected…*with a reasonably fair complexion, red thin lips, eyes that exuded as much eternal commitment as it did incorrigible naughtiness, smile that announced romance – the kind that ruins a woman of her calmness, charm that dwarfed life's problems,* courtesy that would make her his die hard fan, demeanour that would convince her he was…the man…as if the one man she always dreamt about, but knew could never exist, had suddenly been blessed with flesh and blood. Something within her wanted to dance with joy but all she could do was stand by the door, stupidly speechless; waiting for some friendly force to help her come out with the words.

"I said please come in." The man repeated.

"Thank you sir." Swadha continued to stand her ground.

"But why aren't you coming inside? You are the first candidate, right?"

"Yes sir. I am." A cold horripilation ran through her.

"Then do come in. What are you waiting there for?"

Silly Jilly! Move, she told herself and somehow managed to connect to her common sense and ambled forward to take a seat in front of him.

"Your name please."

His eyes were erotically stripping her of pragmatism. Swadha – like a kid – gaped at him helplessly.

"May I have your name please?" He was more assertive this time.

"Swa…Swadha Kashyap."

"Alright Swadha…tell me a little about yourself."

"I…I am a homo-"

"What?"

"Sapien. I am a Homo Sapien."

The man frowned quizzically.

"No, a Homo Erectus." *Help me Darwin.*

For a moment the man didn't get what she was talking about but one look at her trembling hands on the desk and he knew why she was saying what she was. He stood up and came closer.

"Here" he handed her the glass of water that was actually kept for him, "Have this first."

Swadha didn't say a word. She took the glass and started gulping from it. Mid way she looked at him and said, "Thank you." And continued with the child-like gulps. Sometime later the man, with an amused smile on the verge of turning into a paroxysm, spoke up. "The glass is empty now." And Swadha realized she had been gulping from an empty glass for the last few seconds. She kept the glass nervously on the desk.

"Look Miss Kashyap…"

The premonition of what was coming made her avert her eyes. *Silly Jilly! You have blown it all up.*

"I think I'll give you another chance."

Disbelief was evident in her eyes and so was a glimmer of gratitude.

"But only one more chance. That too because you happen to be one of the three candidates that Nitin – the co-owner of the company – asked me to watch out for in particular. Get a grip on yourself and come in after I interview the next seven. You get that?"

Swadha nodded positive and left the room. She headed straight to the toilet. From the time she saw him a funny feeling was alive between her legs. And when she stripped her skirt in the washroom her cheeks blushed to red seeing the sight. Her undergarment was soaking wet.

She rushed to her room in the hostel, changed her undergarment and sat down with her laptop. Seven candidates meant Swadha, at most, had two hours. The previous night she had gone through the official website of the company but this time she was determined to peruse a certain section. In fact a specific name. The website opened – she clicked on the 'About Us' section – then on the Managing Director and a small note opened with a thumbnail picture. Swadha read his name: Haasil Sinha.

She kept gazing at the screen for some time and then sighed in conclusion. *God! I want to marry him. Please no set backs this time*, she added and missed a breath seeing Haasil smiling in the picture.

PALLAVI

Guys and gals lose your poise…c'mon everybody now raise the noise…

A man was rapping in a Caribbean accent as alternating red, blue and green lights highlighted the tantalizing hip shakes and the sexy boobs and butt cleavage exposed boisterously. Apart from the booze, babes, hunks, cocktails and a loud but happening DJ adding motive to the Jam session there was Pallavi, with her gang, celebrating the end of college life. After few hours they sat in a lounge with their favorite Vodka.

"So it ends here!" Priya quipped.

"What does?" Pallavi queried.

"Life!"

"What are you talking about?"

"My elder sis said from here on doesn't matter what we do or however lavishly we live we'll miss this life. Henceforth we'll be expected to do things the way they should be done and not the way we would like to do them. There'll be responsibilities, duties, pressure and all those adult shits! We might continue to dream about this life – alright– but waking up we'll only curse ourselves realizing the dreamt life has already been lived. And no matter how much we crave nothing on earth would bring us back to this life that ends tonight. Not even a get together!"

"Not even a get together?" Riya frowned.

"From tomorrow itself a change will initiate within all of us. Don't worry it won't be a voluntary one. Nor will it be one that we'll be aware of. It'll happen, a little, because of what all we experience from now on and, a lot, how we react to circumstances. We might ring, mail or even visit each other up from time to time but be rest assured we won't be talking like the way we do now. And by the time we all meet up again some of us would already have changed into someone new. Our friendship that looks so beautiful and solid now would ultimately become hollow."

The same DJ who till then was an *uber* sensation for the girls suddenly seemed like creating unnecessary noise. On the hind sight of the depressing talk, Pallavi knew, Priya had a point. But that's not always true, she argued to herself. Moreover none of us are desirous of attaining Nirvana inside a nightclub at three in the morning! So Pallavi did the honors of breaking the philosophical ice.

"Gals, I think Priya is right. Tonight is our last night. So how do you want to celebrate death?" She looked at the girls, one at a time, and each one had a sullen face to offer.

"We" Pallavi glanced at her watch, "have already spent over two minutes mourning in silence over our imminent death. So here's to our thus spent life and whatever that will start from tomorrow. To future." Pallavi raised a toast and after a few seconds of face perusal the others clubbed in. Cheers! To past! Cheers! And to womanhood. Cheers!

"Do you think we'll survive in this man's world?" One of the girls asked Pallavi.

"Of course we'll baby because we are way stronger!"

The girl was shocked. "But my boy friend tells me otherwise."

"Who? Sumit the moron? Okay ask him this: if we women are really weak then why do they need to discharge so many sperms for one ovum?"

"I will." The girl nodded feeling better.

"Now c'mon gals!"

They hit the dance floor together.

The following night Pallavi's parents presented her a graduation gift in the form of a photograph of one of Mr. Vimani's business associate's son.

"Which species does he belong to?" Pallavi asked looking at the photograph. They were having dinner together after a long time.

"Darling that's Jeet. And you are going to marry him this autumn."

"Me? Marrying? This autumn? That too with an exile from the pre Jurassic era? Come on Mom!"

"I have already committed to them." Mr. Vimani's voice had no non-sense.

"Dad, sorry is a wonder word. Tell them that and they won't care about it."

"You know I don't take my words back."

"Then what am I supposed to do?"

"Say yes to this proposal."

"When you have already decided everything does that matter?"

"No. Still I want to hear a yes from you."

"No."

"What?"

Pallavi put her spoon on the plate with a thud, pushed back her chair and rushed for her room and before shutting the door with a deliberate bang, she shouted, "I said no!"

Downstairs, Mr. Vimani looked at his wife. "We adopted her didn't we?" His left cheek flexed sarcastically.

Mrs. Vimani thought for a while and said, "We nurtured her all our life. She is our child."

"Really? But tonight I am forced to think otherwise." Mr. Vimani, too, walked off to his room leaving his wife, staring pensively down at the half finished food, behind. A minute later she got up.

"What do you want Pallo?"

"I want to live my life my way." Pallavi's eyes were red and breath, hitched.

"But tell me in the last twenty-one years did your dad or I push you for anything?"

"So? Is that a debt I need to repay?"

"No!"

"What are you talking about mom?"

"We love you a lot. That's what I am talking about."

"I have seen that downstairs."

Silence.

"Is there anyone in your life?"

Suddenly Dino's face flashed in front of Pallavi. "No."

"Then why are you behaving like this?"

"I am too young to get married mom." She rubbed her eyes and, in the process, reddened it further.

"I was nineteen when I got married to your dad."

"But times have changed now. I can't-"

"So what do you want?"

"I want to enjoy life."

Mrs. Vimani looked straight into her daughter's swollen eyes whose peripherals already had the mark of tears.

"Three years."

Pallavi looked at her mother.

"I'll give you three years to do whatever you want to. And then whatever I say. Deal?"

Through a sulky face a sudden sun of smile peeped and Pallavi hugged her mother.

"Deal. But what about dad?"

"I'll handle him but I have two conditions for you."

Pallavi got up from her bed, stood in front of her mother and bowed down.

"And what are they, Her Highness?"

"You won't take to drugs and you won't get pregnant. Come what may!"

"Your command my obligation, Her Highness."

From the next day onwards Pallavi started ringing up her friends. Some were in Delhi itself and others had already been absorbed at various firms across India. And there were still others who were preparing for higher studies. Pallavi ignored the third category.

One day, couple of weeks later, Pallavi got a scrap on Orkut along with a friend request. It was from Shweta.

Hey Pallavi! Remember me? Shweta here!

The instant Pallavi read her name images of the Mathematics tuition and Dino flooded the love-curfew struck streets of her mind. She did reply back though.

Hi! How are you and where are you? And what about Dino?

Exactly seven days later Shweta's scrap was waiting for Pallavi.

Thank God you remember me! I am fine. I am at Pune now working for a BPO. I don't have any idea about Dino. I searched him in Orkut too but in vain. *So, what's up with you? And do mail me your number.*

It took a second for Pallavi to decide, after talking to Shweta, that Pune was her destination. She packed her bags and landed at Shweta's PG where she was staying with two more girls. She was ecstatic to meet her long lost friend. They chatted the whole weekend. Shweta shared everything from her job to current boy friend while Pallavi from time to time kept harping about Dino's whereabouts with no fruitful result.

It took Pallavi two weeks to find herself a job in one of the BPOs. Though the salary she got, to start with, was only a little more than her college pocket money but Pallavi could afford to be indifferent for she had her mother's debit card. And the day she got her first salary she took all the PG girls to Area 51, a popular pub in the city where her career was about to take a sudden and sharp turn.

"Hey you look gorgeous!"

"Hi! This is Pallavi."

"Thomas. I am the resident DJ here. Ever tried modelling?"

"Not really."

"Oh! You must give it a shot. You got that kind of face and" He looked Pallavi bottom upwards, "Presumably everything else too!"

"I'll think about it."

"Oh! Only buggers think. The rockers only do. I am sure you are a hardcore rocker. Here's my number. Call me anytime." He jotted down his number on one of the tissue papers and was gone.

Back at the PG Pallavi discussed the matter with Shweta.

"What do you think?"

"Modelling is like stepping into lots of shit dear."

"Even BPO is considered to be mud by the outsiders."

"Hmm, you are right. Talk to your parents."

I'll contact them only under gross emergency. "I can't. That's why I am asking you."

"There will be lots of competition. You might have to locate to Mumbai too."

"That's the problem really. Neither do I know anyone there nor do I have enough cash to support me there. I mean I want to do it with my money so that I am not answerable to anyone for it."

"In that case you first work for few more months and then contact Thomas."

Pallavi gave the proposal some thought and then nodded, positive.

Exactly seven months later she got in touch with Thomas again.

"Hey Thomas this is Pallavi here. You remember me?"

"Hi! I am sorry I don't."

"We met in a pub in Pune few months back and you said I had a face for modelling."

"I did? Then I do remember you sweetheart. Where are you right now?"

"In Pune."

"Oh! Give me a call when you land in Mumbai. I am rocking the nightclubs here these days."

"Alright I'll give you a call once I am there. Bye."

Pallavi reached Mumbai the following week and put up at a PG in Nerul with Payal, one of her ex-colleague from Pune.

Thomas asked her to meet him at the McDonald's near Andheri station. Payal told her the way and Pallavi was there on time.

"So tell me." They were sitting across a small table with two chicken burgers in front of them.

"I want to try modelling."

"Try modelling? What is it some junk food? You got to take it seriously baby! Nothing good happens in life without sincerity. I am your man in this field. You have heard of werewolves, right? There are a lot of them in this field. And in daylight you never can tell the difference. But till I am there and you follow my guidance nothing will stop you from rising higher than the stars." Thomas grasped Pallavi's hand and pressed. More tightly than necessary, she thought but nodded, smiling faintly.

Within three days Thomas introduced Pallavi to a photographer who helped her make an attractive portfolio, a *sine quo non* for aspiring models. And whatever meetings Thomas fixed for her soon started producing results. Within five months she started shooting, though on a meager amount, with most of them being ad films for unknown soap, toothpaste, curtains and sari brands.

"Hey Shweta something interesting will soon come in between the boring serials! I have already shot for seven commercials!" Pallavi was ecstatic talking to her childhood friend after two months.

"Great! Can't wait for it!"

But they had to wait. Pallavi did three more commercials but none of them appeared anywhere and when she, out of curiosity, went to the market to enquire about the products only a cold shrug from the shop keepers welcomed her.

"Hey Thomas the products don't exist! Then what was the shoot for?"

The reply came after a pause.

"No worries babes. Will explain it all! Just meet me at Poison by eleven tonight. Okay?"

"Where is it?"

"Bandra, West. Catch a cab."

When Pallavi reached the place she found Thomas already waiting for her. The music, as usual, was blatant. They had to talk at the top of their voice to talk normal.

"What's going on Thomas?" The words intoned suspicion.

"Nothing really. Have your drink."

Pallavi sipped it few times and then looked at Thomas. "Now tell me."

"Well the companies have their own marketing agenda. That's shouldn't be your look out. They have shot the ad and now, when they'll feel like, they'll use it."

"But if I say those brands and companies don't exist?"

"What the fuck are you talking about?"

"I enquired but nobody seems to know anything about them."

"Oh! I told you they all were new ones."

"You didn't say new. You said up coming."

Thomas thought for a while and then replied with a trace of earnestness on his face. "One minute. Let me talk to them." He excused himself. Meanwhile Pallavi, sipping the drink and ordering one more of it, kept panning her eyes. This was the first time she wasn't feeling good sitting in a pub. Her heart craved to be at home. She wanted to hug her mother and sleep on her lap. The thought made Pallavi miss her parents even more. A portion of her was dying to share the experiences of her independent life but the mountain of arrogance didn't let the wind of desire to crossover.

"One more ma'am?" The bar tender asked.

"Sure."

The man obediently bent down, made the drink, mixed the last dose of the rape-drug and serving it to Pallavi messaged Thomas from his cell.

It's done! 15 mins 2 go.

Grt! The reply was instantaneous.

"Hey sweetheart I just had a talk with all of them."

"And?"

"They are having labor problems. It'll take another fortnight to resolve everything and get back in track. And don't worry you'll continue to be their ad-girl! Come on now lets raise a toast to that."

Pallavi, not at all impressed by the reasons, clicked her glass onto his with the drug slowly expressing itself within her. And in the immediate hour Pallavi thought she was flying. Thomas dropped a little ash from his cigarette on her forearm. She knew it was there and was visibly disturbed by it but didn't do anything. Couldn't actually.

Gone with the drug, Thomas jumped from his seat and held her. With the help of the bar tender he got her inside his car and drove straight to his place.

He threw Pallavi on the bed and after adjusting the video camera at a corner, from which it would capture everything, he stripped himself. Next, he stripped Pallavi and thus started a filthy carnal carnage every second of which was recorded by the stationary camera. At the early hours of the morning he drove her to the PG.

When Pallavi woke up, with a heavy and confused head, it was alrea noon. After freshening up she called Thomas.

"Hi. What happened last night? Did I drink too much?"

Thomas only chuckled adding further to Pallavi's confusion. They decided to meet up for lunch.

"Have a look at this." Thomas handed over his Motorola cell to Pallavi. Averting her eyes from him to the cell she played the video. She didn't dare to look at Thomas. After the video was over Pallavi remained quiet for sometime. For the first time in life somebody was trying to get the better of her. She knew what she had got herself into. And what all might or would follow. She could feel her body heat escalating and limbs shivering. One look at Thomas's smirking face and she was back to normal.

"What is this Thomas?" Pallavi said, deleting the video and handing him the cell back.

"Oh don't worry about deleting. I got the DVD at my place."

"But why?"

"Well…one is not a professional till one is bound by a contract. This is your contract with me." He gave her an evil chuckle, "Welcome to the blue film industry."

"I" Pallavi started but Thomas again took over.

"Quid pro quo, baby. Something in return for something else. You'll earn of course. Everyone does. Some with brain, others with body."

"What if I say no?"

Thomas looked at her quizzically. "I thought you are smart enough not to ask that. Look, you got only two options: do it as a sweet baby or I'll make you do it like a bitch."

For sometime Pallavi kept looking intently at Thomas with her insides boiling with revenge. *You challenged the wrong bitch this time*, Pallavi thought and smiled at Thomas.

"I'll do as you say but I got one condition."

"Condition? Really? And what is that?"

"You'll fuck me now in all my senses."

Thomas choked on the cold coffee he was sipping.

There was no modesty from either side since they both knew why they were at Thomas's place. Without wasting a second both got down to work. Pallavi pushed Thomas on his bed and climbed over him. She smooched and bit his lips hard. Then unbuttoning his shirt she kissed his hairy chest and started moving down. Reaching between his legs she took out his belt and in a matter of seconds tugged down the jeans till his knees. She looked at him once and he mistook revenge, in her eyes, for lust. He closed his eyes feeling his hard penis travel between her soft luscious lips. He loved the way she licked and sucked the junior Thomas. *This whore is better than the professional ones*, he thought enjoying the act. A while later he felt something new. He let out a groan first and then a sudden yell as Pallavi's teeth gripped on his penis. Thomas held her head, hollering in pain, and tried pushing her but Pallavi, like an animal on a mission, simply didn't let go till his genitals started bleeding profusely. Few more seconds and, he knew, his penis might be plucked out so he brought his legs into action and tried kicking her along with punching her head. In vain. He moved furiously on bed yelping for his life. "You bitch what the fuck are you doing? Leave me whore! Mother fucker! Oh! For God's sake! Oh! God. Ohhh!" At last he fainted.

Pallavi slowly released her grip. Her mouth was smeared with blood which she wiped with one end of the bed sheet and then spat on Thomas's abdomen.

"You fucking result of a gang rape." Pallavi shouted at the unconscious Thomas. His penis had gone beyond recognition and from now, Pallavi was confident, his orgasm would be about experiencing blue balls. Not an inch more. "Now you'll know what it is like to invade someone's sexual privacy. You-" She kicked his body and spat on it again. "I wanted to pee on you but guess it deserves a better sink. Bloody bastard." Pallavi adjusted her clothes and when her breathing became normal she searched the entire flat with a cold mind. In the end she got hold of the desired DVD, "Here goes your mother fucking contract."

She burnt it right there to ashes and left. Once she reached her PG, Pallavi packed her bags, rang up Shweta and told her she would be at her place by the next day, destroyed her present sim card, left a note for her room mate lying that she was heading towards Kanpur and moved out to catch a bus to Pune.

Sitting on the terrace of Shweta's new PG Pallavi narrated the entire ignominious episode.

"What should I do now?"

"Does he have any of important information like your address etc?"

"No. Apart from my portfolio and the shoot videos may be."

"But they aren't sleaze stuff."

"No way."

Shweta thought for a while. "Frankly, I don't think you are safe here. He must have good contacts with goons and stuff. And considering what you did to him sooner or later he might try to hunt you. And Pune, as you know, was the place where you met him first so…"

"So…"

"You better go home Pallo."

"I told you I can't."

"Oh! Come one. Enough of attitude shit. You don't give that to your parents! You got to move out of here at least. Hey did he know where you used to work before?"

"I think so."

"Then I would suggest you to switch your sector."

"Holyshit! What will I do? I got six months of experience in BPO."

"Look Pallo this isn't just another professional hazard we are talking about. There is a lot of mud involved in it. And you know what happens when a girl's name is drawn into a mud. It will be better if you go to Delhi. If not at your own house then put up with some friend somewhere. At least that's your hometown damn it!"

"And then?"

"Look for a completely different kind of job."

"Ya? Like what?"

"Like…" Shweta shut her eyes to think. "Airlines!"

Another two days and Pallavi headed for Delhi to yet another friend's place in Rohini. She had to wait for four months before the next one-year course batch started at a nearby Frankfinn Academy. After the successful completion, post one year, Pallavi was recruited at Jet Airways. During the course itself she had surmised Airlines would be much more fun than what she did in Pune: helping strangers over phone using a fake name and accent. Though here too there was a certain amount of plasticity but at least this was about faking it high up in the air amongst clouds and not in a stifling office that resembled more of a *sabzi mandi*.

Pallavi adored the job. The highlight was the amorous attention she got – while intentionally moving her full hips or bending down to serve the food and allowing a naughty peep or letting the passengers smell her while placing their luggage on the rack above – from teenagers to young adults to middle aged men to old poops and sometime from the tall and handsome pilots was sublimely satisfying. Men control the society and we control men, she thought and felt, almost sadistically, joyous. Another year passed by. *You got only three years*, her mother's words reminded her time was up. Pallavi was answerable to her mom now.

"I need some more time mom." Pallavi said over phone. She didn't dare to go in front.

There was no reply.

"I said I need some more-" The line went dead from the other end.

Pallavi made a switch to Kingfisher airlines after a fifteen months stint with Jet. That was where she met the popular commercial pilot, Capt. Vikram Singh Rathod.

"I can give you everything except…" He said on their second date at one of the KFC outlets.

"Except committment."

"Well I don't expect that from men anyways."

"I wanted to clear this thing before we hit off." He looked into her eyes, "If we at all, that is."

A man who understands a woman's core never goes beyond one woman in his life and a man who goes beyond one never deserves a woman's core, Pallavi thought and said aloud, "Sure. Same applies to me."

"Why not? And also don't give any emotional shit if I hang around with other girls. Ok?"

There are two kinds of men when it comes to love and committment: one who is honest about his infidelity and the other who is dishonest about it, Pallavi concluded.

"Not an issue!'

The first six months, whenever chance beckoned them, they went to bed together on a regular basis with literally no conversation, only fuck. Next six months there was little talk and lots of fuck. On the succeeding six months they talked more than they fucked. The following three months they talked less and fucked lesser. After that Pallavi heard from Vikram only once in two months and lastly both forgot each other to move on; Vikram with girls and Pallavi with life. And every time, after a tiring night, her heart only had one question for her soul: Would sex with Dino generate the same synthetic pleasure? Or, sharing corporeal privacy with your love is something different?

In the present when Pallavi came back from the pub, draining all her bet money on alcohol, she fell asleep with a hodgepodge of past events stitching her dream. *Do you know what is Ponceo?...Dino has a girlfriend...Pallavi you just signed a contract with me...You got only three years Pallo...My friend's son is waiting for you...she is so hot...can we fuck tonight...This year's Miss Agnes School is Pallavi Vimani... I can't commit to you but I'll give you everything else...You do it as a baby or as a bitch...I love you Dino...Dino ...Dino...Dino...*suddenly she could hear the sound of a siren coming from a distance. It insinuated so much into her dreams that it pulled her conscious out into the real world again. With a confound head and sleep sitting on her eyes she looked at the wall clock.

"Why does it have to show ten every time I get up? Damn!"

For a moment Pallavi lay still on the bed. The television was still on and this time a hospital scene was shown in a serial. With an impulsive change in inertia she got up and rushed to the bathroom. She came out after fifteen minutes and for the next ten minutes kept searching for her mobile phone. In the end she found it in her jeans pocket which lay on top of the to-be-sent-to-the-laundry pile of clothes.

There were nine missed calls and one message. Pallavi cared only to read the message.

Get up pagli. You are on for the Delhi-Mumbai night flight.

She rang up the number.

"Hey Tanu what's up?"

"Do you remember you were warned about getting late?"

"Past is shit. So flush it."

"Interesting. So where are you right now?"

"PG. Why?"

"Move your ass, will you? Only couple of hours to go."

"What are you-" Pallavi looked at the clock again and her eyes almost dropped out. It was ten at night and she had slept for more than eighteen hours straight!

"Oh my fucking heaven!"

"Ya!"

"Could you please ask Dharam *ji* to pick me up?"

"I have done that already."

"Thanks darling! You owe me one."

"Tonight makes it eleven."

"Whatever! See you ASAP. Bye"

Pallavi immediately ran for the kitchen and opened her fridge. It only had one fruit beer, a bun and a small square of Amul butter. She quickly applied the butter on the bun and as she drank the fruit beer she threw it all out instantly. It had gone out of expiry and tasted like poison. Reluctantly, she drank water instead and wearing her uniform in a flash scuttled out of her flat.

Meanwhile Nitin's security check for his flight back to Mumbai had been announced. The business meeting had gone according to his team's script. He missed Haasil, for sure. Especially his knack to guess the client's mind even before the preliminary discussions and also the way he used to charm a client into a positive discussion. As the security official stamped his boarding pass at the security gate Nitin proceeded to collect his handbag and mobile that rolled out from the other side of the scan machine.

Sitting comfortably on one of the seats near the gate, through which the Delhi-Mumbai Kingfisher passengers were eventually supposed to move out and board the air craft, Nitin was lost in thoughts. For the first time after a successful business meet he wasn't thinking about it.

What if my plane crashes tonight? Of course I'll die. But then what will happen to my dreams, the business and Sanjana? Oh! future is so much at the mercy of one single second! If someone asks me to deduct a second from my life it won't matter and still every life-altering incident happens in a second. Their accident must have also happened in a matter of few seconds. And now there is nothing left. Haasil has lost Palki and as if that wasn't enough he has lost her impressions too. I can't even bring her ashes to him. The point is not that we haven't got her dead body yet but how do I explain Haasil all this. It's an achievement these days if couples love each other selflessly and here is my best friend who will have to endure a futile wait. Nitin's jaws suddenly locked tight in frustration. He felt like punching something real hard. *Everything can wait for the time being.* He calmed down. *Right now I need somehow to find a way of covering up my lies. What will I tell Haasil when he next enquires about calling Palki? The truth?* Nitin wondered for a while. *No... I can't risk losing my best friend. He definitely needs time and I...*

An announcement called for his attention. All the passengers were asked to line up in front of the desired gate to initiate the boarding process. Nitin got up, picked up his hand bag and was about to walk towards the queue when he saw a girl coming out of the announcement box. His grasp on the bag, as a reaction, loosened and it fell on the ground. His jaws dropped open, senses numbed momentarily, thoughts froze and the eyes – through the filter of incredulity – remained fixed on the girl. Seconds later he took off his spectacles and for a moment felt numb from head to toe. His heart beats escalated and he, on an impulse, cried out.

"Palki!"

Everyone around paused to look at him.

SWADHA-HAASIL

"NH Consultants Pvt. Ltd is a four year old HR consulting firm. It was started by two fresh management graduates as an entrepreneurial venture. One is Nitin Punjabi and the other is…" She swallowed a quick lump and continued, "You, Haasil Sinha. Though the first year proved negative on revenue scale but the firm hit a jackpot from the time it secured MacInfo – the county's leading IT solutions provider – as a client three years back. Last year it also won India Today Young achiever's award. It is increasing at the rate of thirty two percent every year. And right now it is interested in roping some international clients."

On the first attempt Swadha suffered from verbal constipation and on the second, she realized, verbal diarrhea had caught on. She kept talking till Haasil asked her a different question. Her words kept flowing like a stream of water changing course as and when it hit the boulder of question in its way. The ordeal lasted, as Swadha stole a quick glance at her watch, exactly twenty three minutes and two seconds.

"Thank you Miss Kashyap." Haasil, typing something on his laptop, said.

You have screwed it up silly Jilly! Swadha thought. "Did I?"

Haasil paused to glance at her, "You want to say something?"

"No." She had to squeeze that out.

"Well you can please leave Miss Kashyap. Your interview is over."

Does he have any idea what he is doing to me at all the wrong places...? She looked at him working on his laptop again. *...Or is it the right place?*

Few seconds passed and suddenly he caught her gaping at him.

"Yes?"

"Thank you sir." She left the room and, once outside, sighed in a manner as if it wasn't her career but life that was at stake inside.

By the time all the companies were done with their recruitments – a span of a month – Swadha had three job offers. All were Human Resource jobs with one offering a starting package of 7.5, the second offered 7 while the third, NH Consultants, offered her 6.8 lakhs per annum. Swadha simply tore the first two offer letters and kissed the third one.

"What the fucking frog are you up to?" Preeti enquired.

Swadha only smiled back.

"Have you gone mad or something?"

"I have!" She declared happily.

Swadha, seriously, never thought this could happen to her. Certainly not after all that life made her experience. The truth – in its naked form – lay in front of her since the time she saw Haasil. What if someone, prepared to move from adulthood to old age, suddenly – out of the blue – meets his childhood instead? Swadha was going through such an emotion. She had been in love before – for sure – but now she felt it was only a preparation. This was the examination! She simply couldn't put Haasil away from her mind. Nor she wanted to! Each day, since her interview, went by in a restless anticipation for her joining. She lost all interests in her last semester's project though somehow she managed to pull it off at the right time.

On the farewell night Swadha Kashyap was the one single happy soul in the whole batch.

It took her another week to join NH Consultants and, after fourteen days of an orientation program in a separate office, Swadha stepped into the main office in Mumbai. There were separate cubes for every employee and all the cabins were done in glass rendering everyone visible.

The first day Swadha had a vigilant eye. Office romance is a fashion for many but had-to-romance-that's-why-in-office is rare. Thus, where-is-what and who-is-where became less important than where-is-he. *I'll find Haasil myself,* she promised herself. But no way could Swadha manage to locate him on the first day. Or the second. Not even on the first Friday to her dejection.

On the immediate Monday, while moving out of the elevator on her floor, Swadha dashed against a lady who fell down flinging the files she was carrying into air.

"I am so sorry." Swadha helped her get up.

"Ouch!" She held onto Swadha who took her to a nearby bench and made her sit.

"I am Swadha Kashyap, third floor, HR department."

"Hi! I am Neha. Personal secretary to Mr. Sinha."

"Nice to meet you." And then the last part dawned on her.

"Mr. Sinha? Second floor?" She tried to confirm.

"No! Mr. Haasil Sinha. Fifth floor."

"Oh!" *Thank God I dashed against you.* "I hope you are not hurt much. Look I am really sorry."

"It's alright. Not your fault. I was already feeling weak on my knees…"

A side effect of staying close to Haasil? Can't blame!

"I have fever since yesterday."

Swadha placed her palm against her forehead. *A little indeed.* "A little? You are burning dear." *Nice trick silly Jilly!*

"Really?" Neha was taken back. The thermometer had said hundred and one.

"Let me take to your desk. Then you can relax for a while."

"Oh! That won't be necessary I'll…"

"What else do we work in the same office for? Come on!" Swadha almost pulled her up and placing the right hand over her shoulder took Neha towards the elevator and from there to the fifth floor.

"To the left." Neha was limping while Swadha, apart from supporting her, was eyeing everything with the inquisitiveness of an infant. They entered Neha's small cabin and after helping her to her seat Swadha asked, "You need some water?"

"No. Thanks. And thanks for helping me out too."

"Not an issue."

"I won't stop you here for long. Your work-"

"Oh don't worry! I know my stuff. I'll handle it."

The intercom at the desk rang. Neha picked it up on the second ring.

"Yes sir?"

Oh! Shit! It's him on the line, Swadha thought and it produced a series of goose bumps on her skin.

"Sure sir."

Neha kept the receiver down and was about to get up when Swadha stopped her.

"What are you doing?"

"The boss wants me."

No he'll want me soon! "But you should take rest for sometime. You give me the file."

"Are you sure?" Most of the secretaries have their grey cells in their olfactory lobes. Neha smelt something was wrong. "Won't it be doing too much?"

"What? Forwarding a file to Mr. Sinha? Not at all!"

Neha looked at her totally convinced there was something beyond the normal care for a colleague. "What if Mr. Sinha gets cross?"

"Leave that to me." Swadha winked at Neha, took the file and came out of the cabin. With slow steps she proceeded towards Haasil's room. She could see him talking over the phone in his room. A heartbeat was dutifully missed. Swadha turned right to check herself at the glass partition.

"Not bad." She uttered under her breath and knocked.

"Ya come in."

Swadha pulled the door and stood by it. The door stopper tried to close the door and in doing so hit her back. Swadha stumbled a little in front. "Oops!" She blurted. Haasil raised his eye brows and frowned.

"I'll just call you. Bye." He quickly finished his call and walked up to Swadha.

"I hope you are not hurt."

"This is the sorry and I am really file."

Haasil gawked at her. The correction came soon.

"This is the file and I am really sorry." She took a breath, finally.

"What's your business?" Haasil took the file and leafing it kept it on the centre table surrounded by two sofas.

"Swadha Kashyap. I work here."

"No, I mean do you have an appointment with me?"

It took a minute for Swadha to explain why she was there instead of Neha.

"Look Swadha" He made her sit in front of him on the adjacent sofa, "I really acknowledge this endeavour of yours. In fact it's rare in corporate world. People sometimes skip doing what they are expected to and you…you went out of the way to help a colleague. I really appreciate it. Our company needs such team players." There was a momentary pause after which Haasil continued. "But you also got to understand people are paid to do certain things here. So sometimes we need to forget humanity and respect professionalism. And bright people like you ought to know the difference. Getting me?"

Not a word registered with Swadha. She was lost in his eyes which showed glimpses of that rare genre of happiness that people often run after all their lives with the unlucky ones assuming it all to be a myth while the lucky ones…

"Hello?"

"Ya?"

"I said-"

"I appreciate whatever you said." Swadha lied.

"Good. I am afraid I got some work now so-"

"Thanks a lot Mr. Sinha."

"Call me Haasil. Haven't started graying yet!"

Swadha Haasil Sinha. "Right, Haasil." She smiled.

"See you." He said.

Always! She thought but said, "Ya."

That night the entire sequence of events inside Haasil's room kept boomeranging again and again and again. Each time she reached the end Swadha blushed, rolled restlessly on the bed and started thinking all over again.

It was tough for Swadha to make up excuses everyday to meet Haasil. Few months passed by and she only saw him twice that too while he was leaving the office campus in his car. Helplessly she waited for providence. And it happened few more months later.

At the end of one of the working days they happened to board the elevator together. Only the two of them. He didn't talk and she didn't stop ogling at her target. There was a power cut and the elevator stopped abruptly. The inside was pitch dark and the two could only hear each other's breath.

"Hold on." Haasil quipped.

"Okay."

And in the next instant she felt his tongue on her leg. She swallowed a lump. What is he doing? *Studying you silly Jilly!* Oh! It was coming upwards and upwards, crossing her knees and into her thighs. Oh! I won't stop him even if he rips my clothes off! May be he is the aggressive kind. Suddenly the lights came on. She saw Haasil standing where he was. She shrieked in shock and jumped onto Haasil for support. A slimy creature quickly slithered down her thighs. Haasil, grasping the gravity of the situation, quickly picked up the creature and threw it aside. The endeavour made Swadha forget all about her fear for his hands had almost grabbed her thighs. *Flesh to flesh!*

No comments silly Jilly.

A year later something delightful happened. Or so Swadha thought.

"Would you mind going out with me?" Haasil asked.

Wait! Let me pinch you Jilly babe. Oh! Its reality.

"I am sorry if I-"

"I would love to."

"Thanks. This is for a personal reason."

Love is personal too. "I understand."

"I could have taken anybody but I like you the most."

Ahem! I'll surely die today of happiness!

"And you got to help me out."

"My pleasure."

After lunch Haasil took her to a famous jeweller and bought a diamond ring of her choice and her finger size too. Though Swadha didn't inquire about it nor did Haasil disclose anything but she already guessed his plan.

Hmm. He'll first ask me to select as if he needs to gift it to someone else and then surprise me by proposing with it. Good!

A week later Haasil invited her to his place.

"Are you free this Sunday?"

"I am."

"Mind if I invite you for lunch? Actually someone wants to meet you."

It's his parents. Oh! we are the too fast-too curious couple.

"Sure!"

She reached his house on time. She had intentionally worn Chikan-embroidered Salwar kameez which covered her from head to toe giving her a-girl-next-door look. *What if he has conservative parents?*

The door was opened by an old servant following whom a young lady quickly came to welcome her. She was smiling.

"Swadha Kashyap?"

"Ya." Of course she is not her mother. *Probably sister!*

"Hi. I am Palki. Haasil's fiancée."

A coronary thrombosis. A brain hemorrhage. A nervous break down. A kidney failure. An asthma attack. A complex death. It was a gangbang, she felt.

"Hey thanks for coming. Please do come in. We were waiting for you."

During the three hours Swadha spent with them she learnt they were going to get married within a week.

"Congrats!" *For killing me.*

"Thanks! You got to come."

"I'll try."

"You know the moment Haasil showed me the ring I fell in love with it. Just the kind I would have chosen for myself. And that's when I wanted to meet you. We really do have similar tastes." Palki said.

Swadha nodded. *Yes, we do have similar tastes.* Though the news of the marriage hurt her – a lot deeper than she fathomed – but still, Swadha was in awe of the woman Haasil was going to marry. Palki was sober, sweet, jolly, decent, simple, beautiful – oh! Did God miss anything? She deserves him more than I do for she is better than me. I am…she wasn't getting the word. Hopeless?

"And now I know" Palki continued, "we are of the same nature too. What do you say?"

"True." *Had we been the same you wouldn't have had what I need the most.* Swadha smiled.

Later in the day, when Swadha was gone, Palki confided in Haasil.

"You know she loves you."

"Who?"

"Swadha."

"Really? How do you know?"

"A woman knows."

"Hmm…"

"She is a nice girl. Simple and down to earth like me and with good values too."

"Honestly whenever I see her in office she reminds me of you."

"O ho! So are you considering a change of mind mister?"

"Umm I am thinking about it. But there's a small problem. My kids only want to come via you!"

They kissed.

Meanwhile, Swadha, after skipping her dinner, later that night, and breakfast the next day along with office realized something profound.

Half the headaches in a man's life involve a woman and half the heartaches in a woman's life are because of a man.

I realised it a little late, she thought. But I'll accept it. No bane, no gain. Remember silly Jilly?

As the Stevie Wonder instrumental ended there was a sudden invasion of a haunting silence. Looking at the dark sky above Swadha, for a moment, thought the end of time had arrived. Suddenly her ears started aking in the surrounding noise and she knew where she was. In the present.

The lights of almost every flat were off. Some windows were open while some were shut tight. She could easily hear the footsteps of the guard on his night round even from the top floor. Finally one more day had gone by.

Swadha ambled into the main room, took out the CD, put it back inside the case and sat in front of the dressing table. Till now she had been carefree about the way she looked as long as she was presentable. But now...she picked up a moisturizing cream and keeping her right leg on the edge of the bed started applying it slowly on her smooth cheese-like skin. After applying the moisturizer on all the desired places Swadha combed her shoulder length black lustrous and thick hair. She gulped some water from the bottle kept on the table beside the bed, switched off the lights, adjusted the air conditioner's temperature and lay down on the bed covering herself till her breasts with a blanket.

At least two more months are left for Haasil to rejoin office. But how would I put forward my proposal? *Just don't pounce on him silly Jilly.* She agreed. I'll have to wait and give it a little time. But then till now I have been doing only that...giving it time...perhaps this time I got to take a step. If not the moment he joins but may be soon after that.

Swadha let go an icy sigh and turned sideways. She hugged her side pillow tightly and dug her face onto it. *I love you*, a murmur escaped her.

I love you Haasil...a lot, her mind echoed. *And I don't want to be your hobby...I want to be your habit...* her heart declared.

⌒

PALLAVI-HAASIL

"Palki!"

Nitin, yelling for the second time, ran after Pallavi. Few security men, alert at the sudden out cry and urgency of other passengers, came running. They surrounded Nitin and allowed him to move only after he proved his identity. He slowly walked towards Pallavi who was busy alternating between lining up the passengers for boarding and talking into the walkie-talkie. She was trying to behave normally even though the corner of her eyes told her the man was approaching her.

"Palki?" It was, by all means, a stupid question. Yet he couldn't stop himself.

Pallavi maintained her poise. "I am Pallavi Vimani."

Nitin stared at her face for a while and realized she was right.

"Oh! I am – I am sorry."

"It's alright. We go for sequential boarding so could you please tell me your seat number sir?"

Nitin showed her the boarding pass.

"Please proceed sir."

Nitin, with slow and unsure steps, moved out of the gate.

"Who was he?" Mitali whispered.

Pallavi pouted her lips. "God knows!" They got busy once again with the remaining passengers.

There was another security check before Nitin actually boarded the flight. And through the process Pallavi's face didn't leave him. A hair cut, a change in demeanor and…*even without doing so I thought she was Palki! But even if she resembles Palki how does it matter? Every one resembles someone or the other.* He looked at his watch and sighed with resignation. *Few hours from now and I'll have to answer Haasil. May be this time the truth and then…*his heart suddenly felt heavy. *Oh, God!* Dejected Nitin pulled out a newspaper from the back pocket of the front seat. He eyed the headlines first and then glanced at the tabloid news on the left. Casually, he flipped a page. And then rapidly he flipped back to the front page. The third news heading on the tabloid column read:

SOLAR ECLIPSE TOMORROW.

SOLAR ECLIPSE, he focussed and then only on the word ECLIPSE.

Nitin undid his seat belt, brought down his handbag from the rack above and hastily moved out of the aircraft. It took him another fifteen minutes to withdraw all his baggage and hunt down Pallavi at the airport.

"We need to talk."

One look at him and she knew whatever it was it had to be something as important as his life.

"Sure."

"Can we sit somewhere?"

They proceeded towards the cafeteria.

"What is it?"

"I want you to play the wife of my best friend." Nitin was straight to the point.

For a moment Pallavi was sure the guy was an asylum runaway.

"Excuse me? Marriage? Did my mother send you?"

"Oh! No, I just-"

"I am not for hire!"

"Sorry but I didn't mean it that way. Let me explain." And for the next ten minutes only Nitin spoke.

There was silence when he stopped. Pallavi finished the last bit of her coffee and crushing the paper glass with her hand, said, "So, your friend has lost his wife in an accident. Now he suffers from some form of amnesia. And because I somewhat resemble Palki you want me to substitute her."

"Only for a month or two. Not more."

"What about my job?"

"I have connections. Don't worry about it. You'll be able to join after couple of months again."

Pallavi thought for a while.

"What after that?"

"I told you can re-join the airlines."

"No I mean what about your friend after I leave?"

"He-" Nitin's blank face answered the rest of it.

"If you are in a habit of listening to advice then hear me out. This no way is going to work. Sooner or later your friend will come to know about the truth then why not now? And sooner would hurt less than later. Anytime! You say they loved each other – the type romantic novels showcase – then be rest assured with Palki's demise his life would be like … like…adolescence without hormones, you know what I mean?"

Nitin was still. The possibility of Pallavi substituting Palki, no doubt, was a little fictional prima facie. But nevertheless Nitin believed it was feasible.

"I have my personal life too. Why would I choose to do what you said unless there's some real motivation or reason?"

Nitin, lost in thought, gave himself a faint smile. *When we want to help a friend we want to believe everything…sense and non sense equally,* he wondered.

"I am sorry Pallavi for taking your time. I guess you are right." Nitin, reluctantly sure, got up and was about to leave when Pallavi stopped him.

"Best of luck with it."

"Thanks!"

"Do you have any picture of Palki? I was just curious about her look. You said I resemble her and-"

Nitin opened his wallet and gave her a photograph. "She was more of a sister than a friend." His eyes blurred but the tears were held back.

She looked at Haasil first. "Who is this?"

"My friend."

"What did you say his name was?"

"I didn't tell you his name as yet. He is Haasil."

"Haasil? Haasil Sinha?"

"That's right, but-"

Confounded, Pallavi looked once at Nitin and again at the photo.

"Don't tell me he has a nick name!"

"Everyone has a nick name. But Haasil never liked his so we call him Haasil instead of…"

"Dino!" They said it together.

"How do *you* know?"

Nitin's eyes awaited an answer while Pallavi's got one. The one answer that, she thought, would extinguish all the candles of queries which were lighting, thus far, those corners of her heart which were bruised by the friction of first love.

"Sit down." Pallavi said softly without averting her eyes from the photograph. "I think we really need to talk now."

It didn't take them long, after Pallavi narrated her part of the story to Nitin, to catch a flight to Mumbai. From Saher airport his driver drove straight to Belapur; to Palki's place. And when her father opened the door there was a temporary mismatch between senses and motion.

"Palki!" The name resounded within him but didn't come out.

"She isn't Palki." Nitin said softly, while bending down to touch his feet. He could infer the obvious from his expression. Pallavi, too, touched his feet. Both were ushered to the drawing room where Mrs. Rao was watching television. Her heart froze the moment she saw her daughter.

"I am sorry uncle I came here so late and that too without any prior hint. But as you see" He looked at Pallavi, "It's urgent." Mr. and Mrs. Rao were listening to Nitin but were gaping at Pallavi who, out of embarrassment, chose to look, consciously, at Nitin.

"This is Pallavi Vimani." The introductions were done.

"I met her at Delhi Airport a few hours back. She works with Kingfisher Airlines. And she knows." He looked at Pallavi and then at Palki's parents, "Haasil."

From the time the door was opened whatever Nitin said was a reaction to the facial expression of the couple. Looking at their simultaneous frown, this time, he continued. "They studied together for some time in their teens. Haasil never told me about her."

When Nitin paused and breathed in deeply to calm himself, there was a poking silence in the room. "And now" he started slowly, "We have a situation."

For the first time Mr. Rao cared to look at Nitin. "Sit down. He turned towards his wife, "Make them some coffee."

As Mrs. Rao, more obediently than expected, disappeared into the kitchen, her husband, sitting on the sofa opposite Pallavi, said, "You want to take her to Haasil as Palki, right?"

Nitin nodded.

"Do you think it would help him in any way?"

"I think it would make him happy even if it is for a short time." Silence again. "And as you know Palki always wanted to see Haasil happy."

"Won't there be any legal problem?"

"Only if Palki was alive. I know we haven't got her body yet but we also know the police are losing their grip on this one. By the way, did anybody turn up seeing our advertisement in the newspapers?"

Mr. Rao shook his head patiently.

"In that case Haasil is free to get involved with anyone post Palki's demise. And even if for once we suppose Palki is alive then whenever we get her or she comes back herself Pallavi walks out without giving

Haasil any clue for he remembers neither." Nitin glanced at Pallavi who nodded hoping miserably that such a situation never occurs.

"Do you really think it's easy to substitute people like that?"

"No. But don't mind me saying this uncle but do you still think Palki is alive?"

Mrs. Rao came with four cups of coffee; two black and two with milk. Nobody said anything. They kept sipping coffee immersed in their own sea of thoughts which was producing waves after waves to understand the shore of future. When Mr. Rao kept his empty cup on the table beside him he said aloud, "Alright, I don't have a problem as long as Haasil is happy." His voice lacked conviction.

It was Haasil who opened the door responding to the bell.

"What are you doing here? Where are Jennifer and Raghu chacha?" It was Nitin.

"It's okay! I am alright. How did the business deal go?"

"We clinched it. But where are-?"

"I have allowed Jennifer a holiday and Raghu chacha is in the kitchen. My pains have gone."

"Whatever! The doctor told you to take rest."

"Believe me I have been doing just that and now I need some rest from rest."

Nitin held Haasil by his shoulder and pushed him, jocularly, till he settled on the sofa in the hall.

"Even if there are no pains" Nitin sat down too, "you are still weak. You could have told me about Jennifer at least. Anyways. Tell me, did you have your dinner?" Nitin asked.

"Not yet."

"Then let's have it together."

"Didn't they serve you dinner on the flight?"

"Well they did and its inside me" Nitin touched his stomach, "but I could do with a bit more."

"Sure." Haasil laughed and, turning his head, called out, "Raghu chacha."

"*Ji saab*?" The response came from the kitchen.

"*Khana laga dijiye. Nitin bhi humare saath khayenge.*"

"*Ji saab.*"

Their conversation continued while having dinner.

"I don't think I am suffering from complete amnesia. From the time I cam back to my senses I hear a voice and also at times a face flashes in front of me. But it's vague. Still, I know its Palki's."

Nitin paused momentarily and then, continuing to eat, said, "I understand. Even the doctor told me there'll be some similar problems. Some might prop up now and some few years down the line but if you constantly stay in touch with your past and allow the present to sink in slowly everything should fall into place."

Haasil smiled at his best friend and said, "I don't know how to thank you really."

An amusing smile highlighted Nitin's face. "There is a special way of thanking an old friend. By giving such priceless smiles whenever he comes to you!" They shared a hearty laugh. *It seems like old times*, Nitin thought. And to continue it if I do certain harmless manipulations then I don't think it amounts to anything. Intentions, after all, are more important than the means.

"Is she calling tonight?"

Nitin took a few seconds to answer. "Yes." And he watched his friend's face register a sudden anxiety.

"What is it?"

Haasil shook his head but avoided looking at his friend directly.

"You have been waiting to talk to her, right?"

"Yes. I have been waiting. But now I am having a sinking feeling."

"Why? She is your wife!"

"That's the problem. She is my wife and I just don't know whether I used to call her by some special name - whether we had some love code before we started talking – whether-"

"Relax!" Nitin's mouth was full with the last piece of the *paratha*. "Yesterday I told her everything. So don't worry. She'll do whatever it is necessary to re-ignite what destiny tried to extinguish."

Haasil slowly nodded in appreciation.

"There is another piece of news." Nitin poured some water in his half empty glass.

"What?"

"Palki will be here by the end of this week." *That's sufficient time for me to prepare Pallavi,* Nitin thought.

"Don't tell me!"

"Her agent has somehow managed to book a ticket for coming Friday."

"What's her number?"

Nitin was instantly alert. *Pallavi obviously has an Indian number. He would easily know she is in India right now and not abroad.*

"It's an ISD number."

"I know. We can't use local from Mumbai to America."

"No I mean you don't have ISD on your landline."

"Where's my cell?"

"It was smashed during the accident. I'll get you another soon."

"Till then you connect me to her, okay?"

"No problem at that." Nitin took out his phone and dialed a number. "Ya Palki, Nitin here. Is everything alright there?"

"Hi. Ya. All's fine. Is he around?" Pallavi asked. Nitin had put her up with Sanjana, his fiancée.

"He is. Here, talk to your Palki."

Nitin gave the phone to Haasil who, with a hint of irresolution in his mind, put it against his ears.

"Hello."

Pallavi swallowed a lump. She was about to talk to someone for whom she had cried night after night after night. Someone who had, once, discharged sacred sperms of beauty into the curious ovum of her dreams to make it pregnant with divine hope. Someone who was still her most private desire. Someone for whom she was ready to lose any time. Someone for whom she could win anything. Someone whom she desperately wanted to cut off from. Someone whom she urgently wanted to cling on to. Someone who gave her, though unknowingly, indelible pimples of pains. Someone she wanted to give her smiles to in return. Someone who had once shown her innocence the graveyard of emotions and someone whom, Pallavi realized the moment she heard his voice, she still would give her entire life to say those three words without which the conception of language seems pointless.

"I love you Haasil." She wanted to say Dino but Nitin had asked her to stick to his proper name to start with. Whatever be the name victory was hers.

"I...I love you too."

They were supposedly husband-wife but, Haasil wondered at the slight formality in her voice. *Or is it in my mind?*

"I missed you like hell all these days and when Nitin told me about the accident…" Though Pallavi broke down but the tears weren't part of any skit.

"Don't worry dear. When you'll be here I will surely recover faster."

If she was eventually destined to be his wife – this way or that – then why wasn't she allowed to have him from the time she started wanting him?

"I know." Pallavi rubbed her eyes and continued, "How are you feeling right now?"

"The body aches have subsided considerably and am able to walking properly these days. I am really sorry you had to leave your course mid way to…"

"I can leave my life mid way for you. And it won't be a problem."

There was a sudden silence and she could hear him breathe.

"I'll be waiting for your home coming." He said.

"Even I am dying to be there with you." *We'll share the same house, same dining table, same bedroom and…same bed.* Pallavi in her wildest of dreams hadn't expected this to happen. Such is life, she told herself and continued on phone, "Just take care of yourself and when I'll be there I shall take over. Love you."

"Same here. We will talk tomorrow again. Bye."

Haasil gave the phone back to Nitin who, all through the call, was observing his friend's austerely smiling face. If a lie on his part, Nitin wondered, helped his friend's life to smile this way then – now he was sure – it was definitely worth continuing with it.

Anytime!

The first thing Pallavi did was resign from her job. If it had been a matter of two months, as planned before, she wouldn't have cared even to join Nitin but now – with Haasil coming into the picture – it wasn't two months any longer. *May be the whole life, who knows?* Pallavi felt a rush of adrenaline. *And as far as mom and dad are concerned they aren't coming after me till I contact them. And I will surely tell them everything once Haasil decides to marry me!* Pallavi, suddenly, was convinced about the feasibility of the plan with the excitement of securing Haasil's love suppressing her instincts which told her otherwise.

The four days, following her arrival in Mumbai, saw Nitin educating Pallavi extensively on all the significant details regarding Palki. Even the duplicate of Palki's wedding ring was ordered and delivered within two days. The good thing was they didn't have to care about the minute details or the ones Nitin didn't know for Haasil too, as the situation had it, was oblivious to those.

Meanwhile, whenever Nitin visited Haasil he connected him to Pallavi on his mobile where he saw only her name and didn't care to look for her, supposedly ISD, number. And by the time Thursday night came sleep had completely deserted Pallavi. *One more day and I am going to meet Dino…my first and only love!* All through the night, lying on her bed and smiling to herself, she wondered about the crazy things she did after meeting Haasil for the first time at the tuitions…*scribbling romantic messages on notebook, making hearts wherever possible, writing Pallavi-loves-Dino on every text book of hers, daydreaming about numerous naughty encounters that never really happened, praying for his happiness without any reason, hoping that he did well only because she loved him, imagining his presence in whatever she did in her house be it dining, studying or even bathing…*the funny thing was, she thought in retrospect, what seemed silly now were the most interesting and valuable stuff for me.

By the time Pallavi closed her eyes it was already the wee hours of Friday.

It was around eleven when Nitin's car came to a smooth halt near the main gate. The guard came running comically from his shed and opened it. Nitin started his car again and slowly parked it right behind Haasil's. He turned towards Pallavi, "Your life is going to take a significant turn now. Are you ready?"

"I am ready." The question had only made her more nervous.

Both Jennifer and Raghu were on holiday for the weekend. Nitin and Pallavi proceeded towards the door whereas the guard followed them with the luggage.

The door was opened at the first ring of the door bell.

"Somebody is home!" Nitin smiled vibrantly. As he stepped aside and entered the house, with the guard following, Pallavi stood in front of Haasil. Their common sense wanted them to react but some other mysterious sense took over forcing one to forget time all together and infusing in the other an indispensable wish to hold time captive. *He has become more desirable*, Pallavi thought. *Am I really this lucky?* Haasil wondered. From within they were feeling free but outside there was a stifling air of uneasiness.

"Don't tell me I need to introduce a husband to his wife." Nitin said walking back lazily from the kitchen to the hall toying with a bottle of water.

"Come in." Haasil said. The door was closed by the guard who went away after placing the luggage in one corner.

For the first time Pallavi was finding it difficult to initiate any conversation. While in the car she had been finalizing the possible discourse with which she would start and continue but now all she was experiencing was a black out; a rarity with her.

"I hope there wasn't any trouble in the flight." Haasil asked Pallavi but looking at Nitin. The three of them were ensconced on the sofa with Haasil and Pallavi sharing one while Nitin sat opposite to them.

"Why are you asking me? I didn't come by flight, she did."

They shared a laugh.

"No it was fine." Pallavi said without looking directly at Haasil. "I am only a little tired. How are you doing?"

"Much better."

They smiled to each other. Nitin's phone got a missed call from Sanjana as per their plan. "I think I got to go. Call me if anything's the matter. Okay?" He first looked at Haasil and then panned his eyes to Pallavi. Both nodded with compliance. A minute later he was gone.

Pallavi slowly went and picked up her luggage. Haasil was quick to help her out. She smiled at him and he smiled back. *There is no need of any word,* Pallavi thought, *we are saying so much with our emotions.* She dragged the large suitcase whereas he picked up the two bags and ambled towards the staircase. Haasil was ahead by two steps when he heard Pallavi holler in pain. While dragging the suitcase up she accidentally put one of its wheels on her feet. "What happened?" Haasil turned around, concerned, dropping the bags in the process. Pallavi, as a reflex, let off the suitcase which slipped down the steps while she held on to Haasil's arm in order to balance herself. There was a quick pull from his side which brought her close to his chest and when she lifted her head their lips rubbed against his chin. It made them look into each other's eyes, the second time since her arrival. Her eyes asked of communion and his answered surrender. The next moment they locked their lips tight. Their saliva coalesced and the tongues set forth for a pleasure duel. The hands, with the instinct of children, started exploring each other's body. Love, being the knife of passion, sliced their senses into pieces. They felt like one God creating a new Universe.

Haasil, breathing urgently, picked her up. Though his forearm ached a little but Pallavi's seductive gaze made him forget it soon.

Once inside the bedroom Haasil placed her on the bed gently. He was quick to lift Pallavi's top. And she responded by lifting her hands. As the top came off, and was thrown aside, her hands were dutifully around his neck again. For half a second there was a break in their smooch only to restart again. If the lips were separated now, they wondered, even for a micro second, their lives would get spaced by few eras. And neither was game for any risk. Pallavi knew about dreams turning to reality but the latter turning into the former? She was witnessing it now. Only now.

She brought her hands in front and, one by one, unbuttoned his shirt. Her fingers, at first, played softly with the sparse hairs of his once worked-out chest. He placed his hands behind her which helped him unhook her bra. It opened up and with a little movement of Pallavi's shoulder it came off totally. His hands cupped her breasts. And the first squeeze extorted a vulgar moan from Pallavi.

His thumbs rubbed her light brown nipples that had gone stone stiff. The harder he pressed her breasts the powerful her pull of his chest hairs got and their tongues simply went berserk. They licked the other's face, nose, forehead, cheeks, lips, chin and every corner of the face on offer. Suddenly Haasil got down a little and kissed her throat down to her bosom. He was ferocious but not an animal. He was hungry but not a hunter. He was thirsty but not a traveller. He was mad but he was hers. The ordeal was something beyond Pallavi's experience and contemplation. Fuck – that's what two naked bodies do together; she used to think. But this was not that for she felt her soul getting baptized by him.

Haasil, as if in search of his life's sole purpose, kept moving down. And he got it, after stripping her jeans and panty, at a place which is the gateway to a galaxy where all the magic surrounding a man's life exists.

His warm tongue first touched her inner thighs and made a daring journey further. A long moan escaped her. She held his head and tightened her grasp. Though her eyes were closed she could see what, till now, was invisible to her with open eyes: the sea of heaven. And with each lick her sub-conscious took a dip in that sea and came out afresh.

Haasil took a break for few seconds, doffed both his trouser and underwear together and joined Pallavi again. What she felt, as he carefully parted her legs and gently entered his hardness into her softness, was tantamount to Earth's experience when the Sun's rays penetrated her realm for the first time ever.

Oh! Dino! Her sub-conscious was stifling with pleasure while her conscious spoke aloud in a rasping voice, "I love you."

There was no response from Haasil as he was busy sucking her nubile breasts while maintaining his full hip movement. Each urgent breath of his, sometimes on face and sometimes on her body, was more liberating than oxygen. Each thrust of his was an education for Pallavi.

Now I know why is it so important to go to bed with someone you love. A few tears rolled out of her eyes. *Love is the actual taste of sex. And to by-pass the taste to have the latter – only the latter – is full time foolishness. Of course a plain fuck also generates pleasure but then it's up to an individual's priority: Switzerland or an air-conditioned room.*

Everything outside – as they reached the final phase – seemed moving faster and faster while the inside was subjected to an unusual slow motion. Whatever names she had written in her notebook once, now it seemed, were shouting on top of their voices with a renewed brio orchestrating his hip rhythm. *Pallavi loves Dino! Pallavi loves Dino! Pallavi loves Dino!*

And suddenly she felt the weight of his passed out body on her. She held onto him tight for it was a weight she had been hoping to get crushed by for a long time now.

After few seconds Haasil looked up at her to find Pallavi already looking at him. Both were breathing faster than normal with drops of perspiration glistening with joy on their body. They smiled. He kissed her forehead. She kissed his chin.

"I love you" ...*Dino*... "Haasil."

He kissed her on her lips once and said, "I love you too" Another kiss. "Palki." He completed.

Her heart, at that instant, exploded into a thousand pieces and by the time it rejoined Pallavi, for the first time, realized what her decision to come back in Haasil's life could potentially do to her own life. When she looked at his eyes again she saw in them trust, belief, faith, respect and love of the highest level. She impulsively hugged him tight.

I'll make him forget Palki, she promised herself.

"I missed you like mad." He said.

"I missed you..." Pallavi choked, "like hell!"

It was Pallavi who sat up first. While tidying her hair she heard a subtle music playing from beside the bed. She glanced at the exquisitely designed clock, kept on the small stool, whose silver coloured pendulum was merrily dancing to a tune. It was six in the evening. Pallavi was amazed. Seven hours had gone by and she was yet to unpack! In the first two hours they copulated three times with Pallavi's sexual prowess recharging Haasil each time he passed out. Finally they slept naked on top of each other. Pallavi turned her head to look at Haasil...*her first love ...her husband* ...belief was never so hard to believe. She had only started to smile to herself when she saw something tattooed fancifully on his waist. She leaned forward and slowly pulled down the bed sheet exposing his waist a little along with the whole tattoo. It read:

Palki-Haasil.

Few goose bumps of doubt appeared on the skin of her happiness. Pallavi got down and collected her clothes from different part of the room. She saw Haasil's bathrobe carelessly placed on a chair beside the window. She wore it immediately. Next, she sauntered out of the room, dragged her luggage, one at a time, into the bedroom, unpacked and then went inside the bathroom.

Immersing her naked body in the tub Pallavi closed her eyes trying to relax. Her fears soon caught up with her. *What if Haasil comes to know I am not Palki? But how will he unless someone trust-worthy tells him? And his most trust worthy person is Nitin. I too don't want to play Palki all my life for him. I want to erase Palki and present myself – Pallavi – to him. I am sure he would love me too. I'll do whatever it takes to make him happy. I'll make sure he neither misses Palki nor finds her in me again.* After the corporeal completion, she witnessed in the preceding seven hours, Pallavi was connected to a new Pallavi within. Or perhaps to the old one which was hiding inside for a long time now. Before this she never thought of bowing down to a guy in order to make him happy or gave herself a chance to impress anyone or felt desperate about someone's attention, care and love. But never before was she supposed to be in love either. *Well, I was in love once and I am in love now…but luckily with the same person*, Pallavi smiled. The innumerable excuses she gave herself to forget Haasil played in her mind and they amused her. No one can ever forget – doesn't matter the integrity of the attempt – the person who provides one with a magic spectacle through which everything – from stars to scars – looks congenitally beautiful.

By dinner time Pallavi was doing what she did the best: talk.

"You know I am an expert at preparing Chinese food." She said as they sat across each other while having dinner. Haasil had requested her to make Chinese.

"When was the first time you prepared Chinese?" Haasil said tasting the Manchurian once.

"At ten tonight." They both laughed their heart out.

After dinner they were back in bed. Pallavi, in a silk night gown, was lying on her stomach facing Haasil whereas he was busy describing the after effects of the accident.

"You know I kept hearing and seeing strange things. The words I heard in my dream eventually helped me surmise that someone was waiting for me and that I'd come out of the hospital alive for you. Only for you Palki. I love you."

Pallavi looked lost for a while. When he kissed her forehead she was back to reality.

"I said I love you.

"I love you too." She looked into his eyes, smiled and thought, *I want to win you from Palki*. Haasil realized her philosophical stare suddenly had the twinkle of mischief.

And I'll win you, Pallavi slowly climbed on him, put her legs on either side of his waist and tugged up his vest. She kissed his chest and encircled his nipples with her tongue and suddenly bit him there.

"Ouch!"

Pallavi had a sexy smirk on her face.

"Tell me something honestly." Haasil asked trying to read her intentions. "How much of you is alcohol?"

"First you tell me honestly," Pallavi started moving her hips slowly. "How much of you is a drunkard?"

Everything fine?

Ya!

Since Nitin, didn't want to invade their private space unnecessarily, he messaged Pallavi, every four-five hours, to keep track of events.

Over all he was happy with the proceedings though some messages did tense him.

He was asking about my parents!

Why don't you just tell him they are out of the city?

Ya, I told him they are on an all India spiritual tour. Shall return after three months.

Good!

The next time he asks about them can't I make him meet my parents instead?

We'll see.

Haasil's Sunday morning started at twelve noon. And when he opened his eyes the first thing he saw was Pallavi standing with a red rose in her hand.

"Good morning as well as afternoon sir." She smiled and for a moment

Haasil was confused as to which was more beautiful: the rose petals or her smiling face.

"Thanks!"

"This isn't a hotel and I am not here from room service. I would like you to show me that you are grateful."

"Oh really?" Haasil got up and stood in front of Pallavi. Face to face. "Allow me Ma'am." Before Pallavi could react he picked her up on his shoulder and went to the bathroom.

The brunch that Pallavi prepared consisted of Paneer puff, fried rice and prawns. "When did you make all these?"

"While you were asleep."

"You woke up that early?" He was both impressed and surprised.

"No you woke up that late!" She winked.

It's strange, Pallavi wondered, a sense of belonging does the most beautiful thing to a human being: it makes him a human. There was a time when mom used to literally get on my nerves lecturing on girls-should-know-household stuff and now would she believe her daughter woke at six in the morning and cared to cook for someone?

I don't!

After finishing the delicious brunch they decided to watch a movie on DVD. Pallavi knew what was where in the house. Ironically, better than Haasil. She chose, from several DVDs kept inside the television stand, The Bridges of Madison County.

Pallavi sat on the couch stretching her legs onto the center table while Haasil lay on the same couch with her head on her lap. He was sometimes watching the movie and sometimes staring at her. Pallavi stared at him when he watched the movie but conveniently watched the movie when he turned his head towards her.

Mid way through the film, when Clint Eastwood and Meryl Streep make love while her husband and children are away, Haasil asked, "Its good isn't?"

"Its one of my favourites!"

"I am not talking about the movie."

"Then?"

"The fact that I am a one woman man and you are a one man woman!"

The arrow of words, poisoned with guilt at the tip, hit Pallavi hard and deep. One-night stands, blind dating, sex at first date, swapping men at random, one-timing, two-timing, three-timing and even four-timing for once – she had done it all and without any issue; neither from her side nor from the guy's. But now, sitting beside Haasil, and reminiscing about those days was probing the genitals of her morality; something that never ever happened before.

"Is it important?" She asked with her body turning involuntarily stiff.

"For me, yes."

"But men don't think like you. Nor do women."

"What do they think like?"

"Well everyone is free to find someone with whom they feel like sharing their whole life."

"Of course they are free."

"And in the process if they happen to come across wrong people that's not their fault."

"You got me wrong. What I meant was it feels great to know that we were each other's past, we are our present and we will be our future. People seldom get this lucky dear. You don't know how ecstatic I felt when Nitin told me I knew you from the first year of teen. Whenever I'll say those three divine words to you my heart shall know and rejoice over the fact it never pronounced those for anybody else at any point of time. And the same is true for you as well, isn't it?" He was looking at her. The moment she glanced at him their eyes locked for few seconds. "Ya." It was soft. "But what about people who find real love a little late before which they have already shared a bed with someone else?"

"I don't know. It's complex. Sometimes we don't know we have sex because we are in love with a person or we love a person because we want to have sex with him. It's very hard to decipher the intention of our hormones sweetheart. Reasons-excuses-justifications to oneself after a mistake or blunder in life are important for anybody to move on. But the validity of those justifications, I believe, is pure subjective. And I am not saying dating men or women is bad or sinful or any likewise moral shit. All I am saying is I am super lucky to have you and have only you. I don't need any variety whatsoever!" Haasil looked at Pallavi's pensive face.

"And did you ever think what an example we'll set before our children? They'll feel great to know their father, in his whole life, loved only their mother. And likewise for their mother too, isn't?"

"Isn't?" Haasil queried again.

Don't do this to me! "Ya." Pallavi almost whispered.

He brought his lips close to hers. They shared a gentle kiss after which he rested his head back on her lap.

"Tell me Palki in all these years of our marriage did we ever talk about children? I mean our children."

Though Pallavi looked at him as if she was interested to answer but in actuality she was clueless about any. Nitin had not told her anything on those lines.

"We did…once."

Haasil took her hands and kissed them. "What did we discuss?"

"That we give each other another year or so. By then my course-"

The last part was an unnecessary slip, she realized soon.

"You are in Wisconsin, right?

"Yes. Doing my master's in Social work." Her homework on that was spot on.

"So when are you going back?"

This wasn't part of the homework.

"I" She swallowed a small lump without making it obvious, "I have left the course."

"What?" Haasil sat up. "Holyshit!"

"They were not allowing me to come mid way. So I wasn't left with any other option."

"But…" He was upset.

"Darling no course is more important than you. I love you." She kissed his cheeks. "I'll stay here till you are completely alright."

"And after that?"

"After that I'll marry you."

Haasil frowned.

"Again!" Pallavi added.

Pallavi wasn't allowed to cook that night. They ordered food from a nearby restaurant. And while they were having it the conversation continued.

"I really don't know how I'll cope with the office pressure. Though I want to join this month but Nitin says I should take another month off."

"I want you to promise me something. You are not going to think of anything other than us till you are ready for work." Pallavi had a motherly concern in her tone.

"Promise." Haasil said after shooting a one-cheek smile at Pallavi.

"Excuse me for what I am going to ask you now." Haasil kept his spoon beside the plate and looked at Pallavi sitting across him. She too paused.

"What was your first reaction when you heard about the accident?"

What was my first reaction when I realized it was Haasil Sinha! Her mind converted.

"I didn't believe it. I never thought this could happen to me. I mean us." She drank a little water. "It was horrendous...*it was a miracle when I saw your photograph for the first time...*as if something inside was churning my guts...*the possibility that I can get you back in my life – and how? – choked my lungs...* I asked Nitin to tell me the details and when he did. I asked God why didn't he do that to me instead? *What is His logic behind my wait, behind hurting my feelings, polluting my innocence and then rewarding me with you?"*

. "Hmm. And what did you do all those days? I mean the accident had compelled me to go out of touch."

What did you do all those days when you didn't have me?

I wandered with a destination in my mind but no specific road..."I kept crying for two days straight." *I really did...*"Every time I asked Nitin to get me to you he said you needed some more time. I also tried the landline but Nitin explained the situation to me. And-"

"I understand that." Haasil was done with his dinner. He drank some water and asked, "What if the accident had killed me?"

Pallavi, momentarily, locked her eyes with his. He read horror in them. "I don't want to talk about it." She said.

"Look, I am really sorry. I shouldn't have put it that way."

They were lying on the bed, under the same bed sheet, nestled in each other's arms while the air conditioner was on full swing.

"Do you remember our first kiss?"

"Yes I do." Pallavi recollected their first kiss in the stairs followed up with an unfathomable love making session. "We kissed in the rain." She said indifferently.

"Yes." He kissed her cheek. "The funny thing is Nitin told me about it."

Pallavi turned slightly and kissed him on his lips. "Don't worry darling you won't forget anything from now on." She licked his chin once. "I won't let you."

They smooched for a while. And when it broke Haasil had a question for her.

"Do you have anything to tell me that I don't know?"

Pallavi' senses were instantly alert. "What do you mean?"

"Though Nitin told me about our past but he doesn't know everything. He cannot know everything. There are a few issues, facts and secrets which only a husband tells a wife or a wife confesses to her husband. So, is there anything you want to tell me?"

Yes…that I am not your wife…I am not Palki…I am Pallavi Vimani…we did not kiss in the rain…you are not the only man I have slept with…more importantly Palki, your wife whom you love so much, is dead…

"No, there's nothing as such." She said and a second later felt her lips being clipped by his.

Though Raghu joined from Monday Pallavi reserved the culinary endeavours for herself. From the initial encounter Raghu was skeptical about his *memsaab*. Earlier Palki used to call him *chacha ji* but now she was referring to him as Raghu chacha; just like the others. But seeing his *saab* happy for the first time after the accident and the way *memsaab* was taking care of him – the way Palki memsaab always did – he presumed she was yet to absorb the accident episode.

Jennifer took an instant liking for Pallavi. There was a primal madness in every attempt of her to please Haasil. As if she had suddenly got this chance. As if they got married in the weekend. Well, it's obvious she definitely missed him, Jennifer concluded before leaving permanently a week later.

"It was great to meet you Mrs. Sinha."

Mrs. Sinha! Ah! I like that.

"I want to thank you for nursing Haasil so wonderfully."

"Oh come on. That's my duty but I must confess something before I leave."

"Ya sure. What is it?"

"Seeing you two I realized why it's important to be someone's. I mean only one. You two are made for each other for sure and thank God you met early and didn't have to go through relationship screwups to find him. I found my husband after I went out with five guys! Can you believe it?"

Pallavi only swallowed a lump.

"And now I keep thinking why the hell was I made to waste my time? I could have enjoyed so much more with him!"

"At least you got him!" Pallavi tried to console but was she consoling Jennifer or herself? She wasn't sure. On second thought, she was.

Jennifer smiled and continued, "Whenever my profession keeps me away from my husband I feel like I am losing on life. You know I'll be taking a week long holiday before I join again. As long as one tries to keep the other happy nothing can come in-between a relationship. What say?"

"Absolutely!"

"Sorry to bore you this long. I'll be gone now. You take care and hope Haasil gets well sooner than soon. Bye."

"Bye."

As long as one tries to keep the other happy nothing can come in-between a relationship, Pallavi closed the door behind.

In the next two months a new world opened up for both Pallavi and Haasil. She was over-the-moon just to be with him while he was on the seventh heaven for his wife never stopped surprising him.

"I don't feel like cooking today. Can't we order something to deliver here at home?"

Haasil didn't prefer restaurant food still, reluctantly, he replied, "Alright. I'll order after I take a bath."

And when he came out of the bathroom he could smell his favourite dish being cooked.

"Haasil, I am not feeling well today."

"Why? What happened? Wait let me call Nitin. He can arrange for doctor."

"But the medicine is there in our home."

"Where?"

Pallavi pulled Haasil closer and loosened his trousers.

"Isn't red your favourite colour?" Pallavi suddenly asked, in the middle of the night.

"It is." Haasil was confused, "So?"

He got the answer when Pallavi freed herself from the night gown to reveal her sexy red designer lingerie.

"What did I do to you when you were sad?" Haasil asked.

"You hugged me tight."

"And what did you do to me when I was sad?"

"I hugged you tighter." They both beamed.

"You know why I love you?" Haasil asked while she was busy arranging the clothes in the cupboard.

"Why?"

"I love you because I love you a lot. And why do you love me?"

I love you because you do to my life what I myself would have done had it been under my control. Haasil was expecting the answer he heard in his dream.

"I love you because you make me feel my soul."

Haasil frowned.

"What happened?"

Well, that was only a dream and this is reality! "Nothing." He let it pass.

"You know what?" They were inside the bath tub covered with white lather.

"What?" Pallavi turned to look at him.

"You are so different from what I anticipated."

"Really? What did you anticipate?"

"Well I thought…I mean guessed from your picture that you would be the quiet types."

"Of course I am the quiet types. Just that I talk a lot before I go quiet."

They exchanged a smile and a quick smooch.

"Actually I thought you would never take the first step. You would leave it to me to dig out all the details and set our relationship back on track. And that would have surely worsened the situation."

"What do you think of me now?" Pallavi once again turned her head and their eyes were locked. "I feel happy like never before."

This mean he loves me, not Palki anymore. "I love you." She wanted to faint yelling it but only whispered it, instead, in his ears and bit it hard.

The doctor had prescribed two more months of rest so going out together was not an option. Thus Pallavi did all she could to refrain Haasil from any kind of boredom or frustration. She never left him alone for long. Sometimes they simply slept naked, without any sexual endeavour, hugging each other close and woke up the next morning with the satisfaction of an orgy. Perhaps better! Every alternate day they bathed together. She used to soap his waist rigorously to wash off the Palki-Haasil tattoo but failed every time. That only increased her zeal to defeat Palki and erase all her impressions from his existence eternally.

Each night, after a laborious execution of another *Kamasutra* position on bed, courtesy being Pallavi's experience and knowledge, she used to watch him sleep. This was her best moment of the day. She gazed at his closed eyes, forehead, lips and sometimes, when he turned around, she naughtily tugged down his underwear a little to stare at his cute butt. And once in a while, just to prove to herself it wasn't a reverie, Pallavi caressed her dream, lying beside her, nervously. Of course, Haasil never got to know about it.

During lunch, dinner or at other time of the day they talked non stop. Each word that escaped Pallavi and each time her eyes fell on Haasil only helped her fall more and more in love with him. The way he spoke had the kind of sobriety that not only escalated her respect and admiration for him but also made her feel special and blessed. She never felt the need of portraying any attitude in front of him. Her ego wasn't provoked at any instance. The men she had been with, till date, had love as demeanour but lust as intention. Haasil's behaviour, on the contrary, as much as his naked intentions, announced an eternal communion. Always.

Meanwhile Nitin and Pallavi kept exchanging messages on a regular basis.

You sure this isn't cheating?

Look Pallavi this would have been cheating if Palki was alive.

Will Haasil understand this?

He doesn't have to. We are not going to tell him about it. Jesus! People commit adultery and keep it with them the whole life. We are only helping someone lead a happy life!

Won't I ever stop being Palki for him? Won't he love me as Pallavi? I think he already does.

What's in a name dear?

Sometimes nothing. Sometimes everything.

As of now we should take one day at a time. Don't think too much ahead.

Ok.

And please don't attach any expectations! Expectation means risking unbearable pain.

I know. But tell me honestly who was better: Palki or me?

Dear, ignorance is bliss.

Though Nitin suffered a dollop of uneasiness deep within whenever he, along with Sanjana, visited Haasil but it wasn't showcased in an overt manner.

In the first month it was mostly Nitin and Sanjana who visited Haasil.

"At least you two can come up to Nitin's place?" Sanjana requested.

"Actually the doctor has asked him to stay indoors."

"Nitin's place is indoors only. I mean don't you guys get bored staying at home?"

Pallavi and Haasil exchanged a no-we-don't smile.

"What do you guys do all day anyways?" Sanjana got the answer on her next visit with Nitin.

Pallavi and Haasil were amidst a furious love making session when the bell rang. It cost them their entire will to pause the proceedings. Pallavi got dressed without any second thoughts and opened the door to find Nitin and Sanjana look at her in disbelief. And then an amusing smile took over both of them.

"Ahem!" Nitin cleared his throat.

"Hi. Come on in." Pallavi said.

"Ahem!" Nitin cleared his throat again.

"What?"

"Don't you think" Nitin said referring to Pallavi but talking to Sanjana, "Haasil was wearing this T-shirt and jeans the last time we were here?"

Pallavi got the cue and slowly started taking few nervous steps backwards to reach the stairs. "Why don't you guys just sit down and I'll call Haasil here."

"Where is Raghu chacha?"

"On holiday." Pallavi charged into the bedroom.

"Again?" Sanjana queried.

"Ahem." Nitin responded. Pallavi stumbled into the bedroom only to find Haasil standing like a fool fidgeting with her tiny top that was refusing to move further down his neck and the low waist jeans that rebelled to move up his knees. He paused seeing Pallavi.

"Even before I could tell you…"

From the second month they started frequenting Nitin's place.

"He should start moving out now." She said.

"Absolutely!" Nitin was delighted to see the two of them. He never knew the plan would be such a success. It simply didn't allow his friend to miss his past. At all.

"I guess you were right." Haasil was sitting on the couch while Nitin was busy making a drink for the two. Pallavi was on the terrace with Sanjana checking out her private nursery.

"About what?" Nitin offered the drink to his friend and sat beside him.

"Me being lucky to have Palki as my wife. I believe the most significant discovery or concept in the history of living beings is family. In the end, I guess, it's the status of your family that decides whether you lived a happy life or not."

"Couldn't agree more."

"Palki says I should let go of another few months before joining office."

"Hmm." Nitin sipped his drink and said, "What do you say?"

"I think I'll join by the end of this month. The late I join the more time I'll need to pick up from where I left."

"True enough. In fact I can start giving you a picture of what all is happening in the office. You know our old and new clients, certain new policies et cetera."

"That'll be wonderful!"

"Alright then from the next day onwards we start doing that. Cheers to that!"

They clicked their glasses.

"I need to tell you one more thing."

"Ya?"

"Remember I told you about a voice I used to hear since my hospital stint?"

"Yup!"

"I don't hear it anymore." Haasil looked pensive. He finished his drink and said, "And why would I? I have got her right beside me now, isn't?"

Nitin, instead of replying, preferred finishing his drink.

On the terrace Sanjana and Pallavi, after perusing the nursery, were sitting on the bamboo chairs at the centre of the terrace close to the nursery.

"How is it going Pallavi?" Sanjana knew what was going on.

"It's fine."

"I have a confession."

Pallavi looked at her inquiringly.

"When Nitin first told me about this I was confident it won't work. How can a woman who doesn't know a man play his wife? That's absurd!" Nitin, respecting Pallavi's request, had not shared the one essential factor that lead her to say yes. *Not if he was her first love...not if something inside her craved for him all her life*, Pallavi wondered while Sanjana continued.

"Your parents, relatives, society, friends I mean there so many things with which we remain connected – willingly or otherwise – all the time that every decision of ours somewhere down the line happens to be a response keeping those constants in mind."

"Parents...relatives...friends were never an issue for me. I know what I am doing."

"Hmm. Though having said all that the first I time I saw you with Haasil I was convinced this was the best thing that could have ever happen to him. Especially after Palki's demise."

"What made you conclude that?"

"When I visited your place I saw a person who was madly in love with Haasil."

"Was that a guess?"

"Dear, when a woman is in love, her entire body language changes."

"To tell you honestly even the language of my existence has changed since I met Haasil again." The last word was an emotional slip.

"Again?"

Pallavi glanced once at Sanjana and then at the dark sky above. *A woman can share her past with another woman without risking any blame or allegation*, she thought and told Sanjana about her first encounter with Haasil more than a decade back. Pallavi, because of her own selfish reason of shedding of some weight from her conscience, which from the last several weeks had suddenly reinvented itself, wanted to share more but certain emotional bumpers were so steep that she refrained herself from dolling every event out.

Pallavi, pouring whatever selective potions of her life's journey – deposited in her heart as past – in front of Sanjana, made an important promise to herself, *I'll tell Haasil all about my past too…once I know he is incorrigibly in love with me…only me, not Palki.*

From the next visit onwards Nitin brought some of the office files for Haasil's perusal. He started from the scratch introducing him to the dream they both had, once upon a time, dreamt and set forth to achieve it. Studying the pie charts, power point presentations, bar graphs and all other details hidden in the numbers and the statements documented on the files Haasil felt more and more confident about his joining. And seeing his best friend's professional and personal confidence soaring steadily Nitin relaxed.

Couple of months back I thought it would cost him a lifetime to reach where he is now. Nitin messaged Pallavi.

A woman can make a man do wonders!

Ya! It would have been difficult for anyone to substitute Palki but…you have been the real Jackpot dear!

The word is Jillpot!

Nitin took Haasil to office a week before his official rejoining.

"My hands are turning cold!"

"See! I knew that."

Haasil gave his friend a what-the-fuck look.

"It's your chance to break the ice."

"Break the ice? I think I'll have to swallow it. People are looking at me smilingly and I bloody don't know who the hell they are."

"You don't have to speak all the time. Everyone's your employee. In case you remember anything just do the general hi-hello that's it. All of them here know about the accident but nobody knows about the impact of it."

"Alright."

In the five hours that Haasil spent in his office he met few executives, his secretary, checked out his room, sat there for sometime, talked to Pallavi over phone and during lunch headed to the general cafeteria with Nitin.

"There's a separate room where both of us used to have our food. Remember the room I showed you beside mine?"

"We could have lunched there itself."

"Take it easy. From the coming Monday we'll seldom come here."

They continued with lunch. Sometime in the middle of it Haasil observed a woman staring at him. When he fixed his eyes on her she, with a dollop of embarrassment, continued with her lunch. Haasil, purporting his concentration on food, saw the woman, from the corner of his eyes, eyeing him again. He leaned forward towards Nitin, sitting across him, and whispered, "The woman there" he moved his eyes slightly, "is staring at me from quite sometime now. Am I supposed to know her?"

Nitin casually turned his head, looked all over the canteen, noticed the woman and turned his head to face Haasil again.

"Oh! That's Swadha Kashyap. You met her in the morning."

"I know. But there are other's here too whom I met this morning. They aren't staring at me like that."

"Like what?"

"Like she wants to tell me something."

"Hmm. She has been working with us from the last three years and has been a real asset to the company. Just the progressive young minds we need with us."

"Okay."

"But of course" Nitin had a smile on his face, "That's what I know about her. In case you knew more and never told me then-"

"What do you mean by that?"

"Look at her. She is gorgeous..."

Haasil looked at her again and this time their eyes met. He, as a reflex, smiled faintly while she nervously averted her eyes. Nitin continued, "So may be a little office fling or something."

"Oh shut up! And please don't bring this up in front of Palki."

"I won't. Flings are a man thing." Nitin winked while Haasil, glancing at Swadha for the last time, thought: *she definitely wants to tell me something. What is it?*

PALLAVI-HAASIL-SWADHA

Their lips were locked. Thus, there existed nothing. Absolutely nothing but for the two of them. And because there was only the two of them everything else, they knew, would eventually come to existence, once the kiss breaks. When it did – after several sanguine births and few trivial deaths – the first to happen was the Sun – shinning with the warmth of a graceful grandparent.

Haasil was in a smart black tuxedo and Palki in a cute pink ball-gown. The moment she spun around swiftly on her toe, holding the tip of his finger, a blue sky appeared with few dimples of overtly joyous clouds. She, next, expertly arched back as Haasil's left hand, like a pious promise, supported her shapely back and his right, like a blissful blessing, touched her left thigh that rose a little in the air. The white clouds, seeing the ballad of romance, blew kisses on the couple which fell on earth as divinely delicate balls of snow.

With a jerk he lifted her up again to stand face to face. "I" the instant he started Palki put her finger on his lips and nodded. "Don't tell me about it. Make me realize it." She hugged him tight. Few pieces of wood, lying like orphans on the snow-parented ground, instantly caught fire. They kissed again. A bird, from a distance, serenaded the sequence with a melody that impregnated the air with the prayer of eternal love. Their kiss broke but the hug tightened.

"*What's the difference between a dream and love?*"

"*A dream helps you fight reality by injecting belief in yourself and love helps you embrace reality by infusing hope within the gruesome reality itself.*"

Their hearts were conversing through the language of its beat.

"*Which is more powerful? Love or destiny?*"

"*Though a man is physically stronger than a woman but throughout life he waits for that one woman in front of whom he willingly kneels down. Likewise destiny is stronger than love – any day – but it also awaits the woman of true love in order to experience that ethereal defeat.*"

"*In this era of lies, deceit and adultery how does one make out true love?*"

"*If a single moment or a journey helps you – never mind the manner or the results – find the most beautiful aspect about yourself then it is true love.*"

As their eyes met again the sky became emotional with rain. It was the most amazing phenomenon. Sun, snow and rain – all together. For the umpteenth time the couple surmised why love is nature's most interesting cuisine.

The cold breath of the couple coalesced as they kissed again for, as it seemed, an entire era. When it broke Haasil, with eyes still closed, heard Palki whisper in his ears, "It was great."

"What?"

"That kiss in the rain." This time her reply came from a little distance. Haasil opened his eyes only to feel the breeze hitting him slightly more fiercely. Anxious, he looked around but instead of Palki there were her foot marks on the snow.

Standing beside one of the marks, and looking at the horizon beyond,

Haasil yelped with all his might. "Palki, where are you?"

You know something Haasil – a voice shot back from exactly where he didn't know – *the most amazing love story happens between life and death. Both have only one purpose in their core: to meet the other; sooner or later.*

Confused, Haasil chose to follow the foot prints on the snow which lay on the vast landscape like innocence upon childhood. The foot prints, once every while, finished abruptly arousing his desperation. Relief came when the female voice came to him again tearing the apparel of the sky.

"On the globe of my heart there's only one ocean and only one continent: Haasil."

And the moment the words hit his ears another set of foot prints appeared in an entirely different direction. He followed till they no longer existed after a distance.

"It's not about the picture but about each of those single pieces that make it...one single piece...one single day...if you take care of the pieces and if they are right then the picture ...the relationship...will adjust itself to perfection."

The chase for the desired destination started again.

"Love is the conjunction between the sentence of life and purpose."

Finally, at the end of a series of foot prints, he saw someone standing with open arms. She had put on Palki's gown. As her face became prominent he didn't believe his sight. *It can't be her!* But his confusion only escalated as he ambled towards the figure.

"My wait is over." She cried. "Come to me Haasil."

"You-" He pointed his finger at her but before he could complete Nitin's words resounded in his mind.

"Oh! That's Swadha Kashyap."

Haasil sat up with a start as if an express train had suddenly braked. His heartbeats were racing, the sweat glands hyper active and his senses grossly strained. Pallavi was quick to switch on the bed light. She held him steady and caressed his forehead rubbing the perspiration with her palm.

"What is it darling?"

"I" He looked at her confused. "I don't know. There was this woman-"

"Wait." She turned and picked the bottle from the table beside the bed and gave it to him. "Here drink some water first."

With his breaths trotting back to normalcy Haasil gulped half the water. He gave the bottle back to Pallavi and took a deep breath.

"Are you feeling alright?"

"Somewhat."

"You were saying something."

Haasil looked at Pallavi once. "Yes."

"What is it?"

"I saw myself following some foot prints leading to a woman."

"Then?"

"I saw her face."

"Who was she?" Pallavi asked feeling a lump in her throat. *Is he getting back his memory?*

It was Swadha Kashyap. The one I saw in office. But would Palki react positive when she hears it? He thought but said aloud, "I don't know."

"Okay no need to stress yourself. C'mon lie down now." Pallavi switched off the light and holding Haasil gently rested on the bed again.

Do I really have something to do with Swadha? Affected by the dream Haasil closed his eyes.

Though Pallavi closed her eyes too but her mind was wide awake studying a question. *I am sure he knows the woman. But why would he lie? If only the woman wasn't...me.*

Swadha, by far, was the happiest to see Haasil back in office. And this time things seemed more auspicious than before. *He glanced and even smiled at me once!* She was totally drugged with love.

There were few questions too. *He looks as much relaxed as confused. Didn't the loss of his wife upset him? And why was Nitin showing him everything in a way as if he was new to his own office?* Just when Swadha's intellect was about to raise the curiosity alarm an old voice inside her spoke up. Rather rudely. *Silly Jilly! On one hand you keep cringing whether God at all has made any one for you and when you have him smiling at you instead of reveling in it and finding ways of carrying this beautiful initiation forward you are harping on why he did so? Well, now you know why you have been single till date! Girls like you...*

Stop! The only thing that matters to me is he smiled at me. Yes he smiled at me! That's a start. Everybody has their share of good and bad luck. And my good luck is just here!

That's better! She heard the voice again and for the umpteenth time indulged in the reminiscence of whatever happened in the canteen.

Haasil, as scheduled, officially joined NH Consultants officially on the immediate week. The office hours went by without much of a hullabaloo. He was in his cabin most of the time and lunched with

Nitin in their private space. After the working hours a small welcome soiree was arranged in Haasil's name by the employees in the office banquet hall with all the staff attending it. Swadha, more importantly, was there. Her attempt to take extra care while dressing was supremely evident. A white shirt, whose first two disengaged buttons allowed a peep onto her sweet cleavage, an off-white pearl necklace that helped accentuate the cleavage's sensuous appeal, a cream coloured business suit with a matching pencil skirt serving her intention to outline the nubile portions of her hips to perfection, on one side her open hair was carefully tucked behind her ears so that at least one of the sparkling pearl ear-rings was constantly visible. The cynosure of her appearance, though, was her lip-gloss embellished smile in which some of the males found the essence of a high quality Viagra.

But Swadha claimed her endeavour as successful only when Haasil's eyes met hers in the party. This time she smiled and he reciprocated. *He smiled too!* And waved his hand towards her. *A wave of hand!* In order to negate any chance of suffering from a reverie and prove to herself that Haasil was actually waving at her – only at her – Swadha thought of a ploy. She mingled in the crowd and was soon out of his sight. Peeping over the shoulders of few she could see Haasil. It was evident from his body language he was trying to locate someone. *Me?* Her personality inflated with pride because she wasn't available easily to him. *Let him search a little longer.* She was enjoying the tease when suddenly a voice said, *Silly Jilly! He is trying to find you and you are playing games with him? What if he finds someone better than you? You keep hiding and go to hell.*

Sorry! Swadha ejaculated softly to herself, cleared her throat and took a deep breath before proceeding towards Haasil with a throbbing heart. When she was few steps away from him he turned his head casually to look at her.

"Hi!"

"Hello. How are you doing?"

"Fine." Everything was coming out with halo of nervousness.

"Where did you vanish all of sudden?"

So he was looking for me! Oh! He was! "Drink!" Swadha raised her hand which didn't have any glass.

"I- I mean I went to keep the glass. I have had enough."

"I see. And thanks."

"For?"

"For such a lovely welcome."

"How did you-"

"Nitin told me. You spread the idea amongst the staff."

"I thought you'd like it."

"Of course I do."

The idea or me? "Thank God!" She smiled. And suddenly the dream flashed before Haasil's eyes where she was calling him with open arms and with that same life-enduring smile on her face.

"I hope you are perfectly fine." The words broke his trance.

"Huh?"

"I hope you have recovered from the accident."

"Oh! Yes. There's a fine line between life and death. Glad to be still on the right side."

"True. In fact the most amazing love story happens between life and death."

"Hmm...well said."

Nitin called out Haasil's name and he gesticulated to him with a give-me-a-second look.

"I am sorry but you got to excuse me."

"Oh! That's not a problem." She was heart-broken. The conversation was helping all kinds of pleasure hormones explode into her blood stream.

Haasil turned around, kept his empty glass on the tray offered by a nearby boy, picked up another glass and ambled towards Nitin with his mind recapping Swadha's analogy.

"In fact the most amazing love story happens between life and death." He paused. And frowned.

The most amazing love story happens between life and death. Both have only one purpose in their core: to meet the other; sooner or later.

He recollected what the mysterious voice told him in his dream. What the hell? How did she know it? Haasil, sustaining the frown, glanced at Swadha once. She was still looking at him. *Again, the same smile.* For a moment, their conscious was captured within the concrete capsule of a mystic force which tranquilized their present to allow them a glimpse at the two sides of the coin of time: He, staring at her, tried to decipher his past. She, gaping at him, tried to read her future.

"Sorry ma'am." A callous dash by a colleague against Swadha's shoulder brought her back to reality. She immediately stopped smiling. And as the smile dried Haasil too was back in the party atmosphere. She could read his eyes. The emotional alphabets it contained were known to her but the language wasn't making sense. Yet.

He too has something in his mind. But, what is it?

Haasil avoided talking about the party incident with Pallavi. "First let me sort it out myself then I'll let Palki know about it." He promised himself seeing Pallavi at the doorstep after he came back from office that day. Though he didn't dream anything the succeeding night but it was Swadha's smile that eventually lulled him to sleep.

Next day in office, while his secretary was leaving the room, explaining him the day's itinerary, Haasil stopped her with a question. "Neha, did Swadha submit any file?"

Neha turned around with squinted eyes and stood recollecting all the morning happenings. "No she didn't. Should I-"

"Never mind. Could you please ask her to come over?"

"Sure!" She was gone.

The intercom was picked up at the second ring.

"Swadha? Were you supposed to submit a file to Haasil?"

Was I? No! "Why?"

"He wants you in his room. Now."

He wants me? The pun, though unintended, tickled her senses. "Oh! I remember now. Yes I had to submit one." She lied to avoid unnecessary deductions. "Thanks for reminding."

"My job."

Keeping the receiver down Swadha pushed her chair and sprang into action. Action one: go to the washroom. Action two: mirror! Action three: check your suit, hair and make up. Action four: Take a deep breath and take is easy. Action five: Haasil's room.

"Come in please." Haasil responded to the mild knock on the door. Swadha stepped in.

"Good morning Haasil."

"Good morning. Please have a seat."

Relax silly Jilly! Swadha carefully moved ahead, pulled one of the chairs and sat on its edge. "Thanks."

"Sorry to call you like this."

Sorry? Only if you knew what it means to me. "Not a problem. Neha told me about some file. But-"

"Forget that…"

*I knew it was an excuse. He wanted to meet me, see me and…*she heard him continue. "Yesterday you said something about life and death being an amazing love story. You remember?"

"Ya."

"Where did you get that from?"

Swadha didn't realize her mistake when she uttered it the last evening but now the significance dawned upon her.

"I am really sorry for that."

"For what?"

"Actually, Palki had once told me about it…"

Alright! I was thinking all kinds of neurotic things, Haasil sighed.

"And I am sorry for mentioning it and also her name now."

"Why should you be sorry? She is neither an outcaste nor a national villain!"

"No I mean…"

"Oh bunk it! Do you remember the time when you met her?"

Do I remember? Mr. Haasil I cried my heart out that day. "Well don't you?" Swadha asked back.

"I-I do. Of course!" Haasil stammered out in defence. "Its amazing that you remember such minor things. I am pathetic at it sometimes." He was only killing time now.

Meeting the woman who had my dream man…a minor thing? It was like the surgeon of life operated on my wounds with all my senses awake. "It was quite an interesting meet. Perhaps that's why it stuck on."

"Perhaps."

"By the way" she moistened her lips, "did you call me just to discuss yesterday's statement?" *Fortune deavours the brave.* She missed a beat.

Silly Jilly it's fortune favours the brave! The correction relaxed her.

"No." *What should I tell her now?* "Actually I called you because…" *think of something…* "I wanted to tell you something."

Swadha felt an instant thud in her heart and twitch in her thighs. She budged on her seat. *Is he proposing?* "What is it?"

"No, I wanted to ask you something." Haasil was impulsive.

Is he going to ask me out? "Ya, what is it?"

"Sorry, I think I'll request."

Oh! Come of it now! "Please."

"It would be great if you come up for dinner at my place."

"Sure." The reply was prompt. Haasil heaved a sigh of relief. *Matter well handled!* Prior to the accident he was, as Nitin told him, articulate, assertive and analytical with all his discourse. And now every time a conversation struck he had to push himself hard to steer it to his liking. *Has the accident taken it all from me?*

Meanwhile. Swadha was forced to listen to the voice with serious attitude problem. *Silly Jilly! Don't say yes like a love slave. Let him request you more…let him crave and get down on his knees!*

"I mean are you sure about this?"

"Yes. You know both of us. And we know you. So what's the formality about?"

But Palki is no more. Swadha forwent reminding Haasil about it. Someone who is gone is gone. No use mentioning her name all the time and awake the pain that the conscious so frantically wants to bury inside the graveyard of the sub-conscious. *Moreover Palki's name in our discussion might hinder my love story,* Swadha thought and said,

"But at your place?" *Only you, me and our tacit emotions. Wow!* "Don't you think eating out is a better idea?"

"We can eat out some other time as well. I don't like going out that much. But in case you have a problem its okay. It's not any professional obligation mind you."

Catch him! Enough of teases! "No no it's okay with me. I'll be there. Tonight?"

"Not tonight." *I need to consult Palki too.* "But I shall let you know."

No matter how much situations try to suck out hope our love for someone should never leave its adolescence. Till yesterday he was a dream for me but now he wants to dine with me. Swadha's love finally felt blessed. Lovers will grow old – can't help it – but their love should always remain corked within the bottle of vivacity perennially securing its joyous effervescence, she wondered and said, "No problem."

"Thanks." Haasil said and thought, *there's something about her that reminds me of someone. Don't know but I think I like her. She's sweet…and sexy in her own way.*

Pallavi was getting late with the final chores of the day. Haasil, lying idly on his bed, was waiting for her. With the tick of each second he was impatiently flipping a page of the *Business World* magazine.

From the moment Swadha had left his room in the morning he wanted to discuss a few things with his wife and had intentionally chosen this part of the night for doing so. And when Pallavi finally stepped into the room he welcomed her with a rich smile. "Everything's done?"

"Yes dear. Was explaining a few things to Raghu chacha." Pallavi first checked her hair in the full length mirror and then ensconced beside Haasil pulling the bed sheet onto their bust. She closed the magazine for him, kept it aside by her pillow and was about to turn off the lights when Haasil stopped her. "One minute."

Pallavi looked at him inquiringly.

"Do you know any Swadha Kashyap?"

It was a catch-twenty two for Pallavi. *Whatever I say — yes, no or even an I-don't-know — is a risk.*

"Why are you asking? What happened?"

"I had a talk with her in the office today." At first he thought he would like a face to face discourse. But changing his mind he chose to switch off the light himself. Adjusting his pillow he lay down straight.

"I had a talk with her yesterday also."

Pallavi budged uncomfortably and looked at his subtly visible face in the dark.

"During the welcome party?" She guessed.

"Yes." The word came out as a whisper. It gave way to a silence that neither of them chose to break for several minutes. Until the silence stifled one of the two.

"That night I lied to you." Haasil said. "I dreamt of Swadha. But believe me I really don't know why." The voice rose in the beginning but softened later. "Yesterday she told me something about life and death that reminded me of the dream I used to have in the hospital." Pallavi turned her profound face towards the ceiling now. "Today when I asked her about it she told me you'd once shared the thought with her." A hiatus. "When was that?"

Pallavi's heart, anticipating the worst, was already galloping towards a consuming fear. *Has Swadha told him more than what is necessary? Does she know Palki is dead?*

The delay in the reply emboldened Haasil to turn towards Pallavi. He kept his hand across her belly and asked again, "Hey dear" he caressed her navel slightly, "When did you meet Swadha?"

"It was – it was before I went abroad."

"Hmm. She is a nice girl. I like the way she carries herself." *Different from Palki.*

Pallavi's within was not appreciating a bit of what was going on. "Ya" she said with reluctance dipped in sarcasm, "she is a sweet girl."

"I want to call her for dinner tomorrow. Is that okay with you?"

Pallavi, suddenly, locked her jaws and her entire body momentarily turned stiff with annoyance. "It's perfectly alright darling." She didn't know how the words escaped her but she was glad they did else it would have made Haasil suspicious.

"Thanks." He said and kissed her cheeks once.

"I know she likes you." Haasil further said, "The way she talked – whatever little bit – it had respect. I hope you like her too."

"Ya! A nice girl. I like her too."

"By the way what made you meet her?"

"Umm…don't mind dear but I really don't remember specifically."

"Oh! Never mind." Haasil pulled her closer. Another silence followed. People call it silence but sometimes it makes the maximum noise within. Pushed by such a noise Pallavi asked straight, "Tell me Haasil, is Swadha more beautiful than me?"

And in reply she got the sound of a soft yet consistent snore. Realizing he was asleep Pallavi, with the demeanour of a thief, took his hand away from her and climbed down the bed. Picking up her mobile phone from the dressing table she walked out of the bedroom. Before reaching the staircase she had already dialed Nitin's number and by the time she sat on one of the steps the call had started.

"Pallavi? At this hour? Everything's fine?"

"Can you hear me?" She was whispering into the phone.

"Ya but what's the matter?"

"Who's Swadha Kashyap?"

"Where did you get her name?"

"Haasil told me about her. She has met Palki before. And she is coming to dinner tomorrow."

"But I don't think she knows about Palki's death."

"Are you sure?"

"Umm…I am but then" After a pause he added, "you never know. Now wait a second Amit knows about Palki's death. He had accompanied me to the hospital after the accident. But I've already told him about you. He is my closest after Haasil. And he understands the situation perfectly."

"May be an ignorant slip on his part…"

Nitin thought for a while. "May be."

"So what do we do now?" Pallavi was tempted to repeat her query when she heard him speak.

"I need to tour a few places starting tomorrow night."

"Like?"

"First Delhi then Bangalore and lastly Singapore."

"And you want to take Haasil with you?"

"That's a stop-gap. It'll keep him away from her and won't expose us to any untoward risk. After we return we'll think of something more concrete, what say?"

"Alright. You let Haasil know about the trip, okay?"

"Ya. Don't worry. I'll do that tomorrow morning itself. Get some sleep now."

"You too. Bye."

As the call ended Pallavi stood up and ambled towards the bedroom. But before entering it she messaged Nitin.

You really think our means of keeping Haasil happy is right?

The reply came only after Pallavi had retired to bed, the second time, beside Haasil.

At least our intentions are right. Rest, God knows.

It was in the first hour of office, the following day, Nitin talked about the trip.

"You should start taking these tours now. We'll be a team of five. I'll handle the work but I think your presence would be fruitful for both our company and yourself."

"Ok! What's the schedule like?"

Whatever Nitin told him was dutifully relayed to Pallavi.

"I'll be gone for twenty days or so. Delhi-Bangalore-Singapore and back. Will you please do the packing for me? I am on for tonight's fight."

"That'll be done. I hope it won't stress you."

"I have already lost ample time. Now I need to push myself for the company's sake."

"I understand."

There was neither a chance nor any plausible reason for Haasil to let Swadha know about the tour. *My extra concern might be interpreted otherwise. Moreover she'll, anyways, come to know about my absence eventually. And once I am back I can always invite her for dinner again.*

The next twenty days saw Haasil coming closer to work and understand the ongoing business scenario better. Nitin took the final decision at all the client meets but only after discussing every aspect with Haasil first. The meetings that happened in each of the three locations added range to Haasil's numbed business acumen. In Delhi, they met one of their top clients, Sky Tech Incorporation, to devise a fresh strategy to prune the company's work force because of the emergence of sudden world recession. In Delhi, again, they also met up with the executives from Demon Images Pvt. Ltd, an advertisement agency, to strike a deal of getting their human resource issues outsourced to NH Consultants. In Bangalore, a five day meeting with the BPO branch of Cranium Inc. happened and certain futuristic decisions were made to curb specific HR costs. A one day out of schedule trip happened to Pune where they attended a Leadership Summit program organised by a leading daily. Finally they flew to Singapore which was more about giving wings to NH Consultants expansion plans.

Every night, after being enlightened by a *de novo* facet of business during the day, Haasil craved to hear Pallavi's voice. And it was a mutual feeling. Though Pallavi herself was a part of the plan that made Haasil travel but once he was gone, she realized, no matter how earnestly she explained to her heart about the urgency of such a ... there were certain portions that continued their immature rebellion.

Positive change is growth. Haasil's coming back to her life had imbued just that within her – growth. Some of the things she did earlier – and sometimes all of it – now seemed meaningless and trashy. Things which she once considered to be fun and not-a-big-deal now tantamount to cheap ways of insulting a beatific gift called life. Haasil's love definitely was a sleeping pill for most of the noises inside her mind that compelled her earlier towards a self-degrading process. The biggest miracle one can witness in life is, perhaps, the process of binding of the heart and soul. That's when individuals realize their true identity. Pallavi never believed this could happen to anyone. Not her at least.

"Missing you like hell cutie."

"Same here. Only one more day."

"Ya!"

"Did the last seventeen days consist of hundred hours a day?"

"You bet!" They shared half a minute of laughter.

"You know sometime I feel scared."

"Why?" Her tone turned somber.

"I have got a great friend, a splendid wife, a promising company and everything else a man usually aspires to have. I don't want to lose it at any cost."

*A splendid wife…*what is it? A stab or a pat? Pallavi wondered.

"You there?"

"Ya, sorry…you don't have to be scared dear. I'll be with you always."

"I know." A hiatus. "I love you."

"I love you too." And only she knew how little of her love was packaged in those three words.

When the call was over Pallavi kept the cordless back on charge. The desk calendar, precisely then, netted her attention. Haasil would be back on 21st. *Oh!* It suddenly struck her. It's his birthday! She immediately messaged Nitin.

You free? Need to talk.

The next minute Nitin called up.

"Any problem?"

"The day after tomorrow is 21st. Haasil's birthday."

"Hell, I almost forgot."

"Mind if I arrange for a little party at home?"

"Not at all. In fact that would be great for him."

"Okay but let this be a surprise."

"Ya, sure. What about the arrangements?"

"Leave that to me."

The following day Pallavi spent the morning session planning. She not only wanted to surprise Haasil but also, steadily, wipe out Palki from his life. And if all these days of communion were a preparation than this party, she thought, would be the first step towards that dream. It wasn't a jealousy issue. It was worse. She felt irreversibly defeated whenever he said 'I love you, Palki'.

But Pallavi can never lose, she was confident.

The first thing in contention for the party was the caterer. She, with reference from Sanjana, rang the best caterer in town and fixed them for the party. In the evening she went shopping. Armani, Tommy Hilfiger, Marks n Spencer, Panache, Victorinox, Chivas, Louis Philippe; nobody was spared. She bought herself a red gown, a few bottles of French perfume and later ordered a three storey Swiss chocolate cake. After placing the order her eyes chanced upon the fountain of chocolate. A mischievous idea beckoned her. This could be part of the party Haasil and she could enjoy in bed after the guests were gone, she thought, and bought ample amount of chocolate sauce and several bars of dark chocolates. The idea also made her purchase some red heart-shaped love candles. He won't forget this birthday; Pallavi blushed reacting to certain erotic images the idea torch-lighted on her mind.

While moving out of the shop one of the candles popped out of her bag. The man beside her picked it up for her.

"Here."

"Thanks." She was gone.

The man, without losing a second, dialed a number on his mobile phone and, as his eyes followed Pallavi moving down in the escalator, he spoke. "I just saw Pallavi Vimani."

"Who?"

"Pallavi Vimani." Each word was stressed.

"What? Where?" There was jubilation in the voice.

"In a mall." The man was alternating between movement and pause. He wanted to keep a track of her without making it obvious.

"Are you sure it's her?"

"Swear on her mother's pussy."

"And if she is not…"

"Castrate me!"

"Alright. Now follow her damn it. And find out where she is putting up. I want to know everything about her. Got me?"

"Ya. I'll call you back." The line went dead.

I knew I'll get that bitch one day… Thomas murmured to the prostitute lying beside him naked on bed massaging his groin. He suddenly hollered, "Slowly you cock sucker! Someone bit me there once. And it still pains."

Nitin, after they were done with the breakfast, gifted Haasil a Parker pen.

"Anything special today?"

"Nay!" Nitin lied with a smile.

"At what time is the flight?"

"We are flying first to Delhi. We got to attend an important meeting there. It'll take an hour and then we'll fly to Mumbai."

"Is it an emergency?"

"Sort of."

"Alright let me call Palki."

"Sure. And I'll pack up." Nitin disappeared into his room as Haasil rang Pallavi.

"Hi!" She was dying to wish him but held on to protect the spirit of surprise.

"Dear I'll be home by night."

"Night? What happened?"

"An urgent meeting has cropped up in Delhi. So we'll be going there first and catch a flight back home later."

"Hmm, okay." Her disappointment was evident.

"I am really sorry baby."

"Oh it's alright. Work first."

"Thanks. Love you!"

"Love you too my life. Come soon, someone's waiting!"

After their Air India flight touched Delhi's chest in the afternoon they went to Centaur to attend the scheduled meeting. It took a little more than an hour after which they proceeded towards the airport to catch their Kingfisher flight in the evening. By the time Haasil and Nitin were walking towards the luggage corner it was already nine.

The moment they stepped out, pushing their trolleys burdened with the belongings, both of them found their respective drivers waiting.

"I'll call you once I reach home. Take care buddy." They hugged. Nitin got into his Chevrolet and left. *A quick shower and then party time*, he thought and knew Sanjana must be waiting for him, all dressed up.

As Nitin's car sped off, Haasil, watching his driver placing the luggage properly behind, got into his Toyota. They were driving out of the airport premise when he suddenly quipped, "*Ek* minute!" He peeped out of the window frame and frowned. Once he was sure of the person's identity he got down and approached her.

"Hey! What are you doing here?"

Swadha, for a trice, didn't know whether it was a reverie or reality. Throughout the day she'd been thinking about him. *It's his birthday!* She knew and longed to wish him from twelve o clock itself but now, when he was there in front of her, Swadha suffered a blackout.

"Hello!"

"Oh! Sorry. I mean what are you doing here?"

"I think I asked that first."

"Sorry. I had gone home to Lucknow the day before yesterday. Dad's a little sick."

"First tell me are you waiting for a taxi?"

"Ya. I had taken one but its tyre went burst. And now I am not getting any."

"No problem. I'll drop you to your place."

"No, that won't be necessary." *If he asks once more I'll agree.*

"Where do you stay?"

"Versova."

Haasil consulted his driver quickly.

"That's a little far from my place. Why don't you come down with me?"

"Where?"

"To my place."

"Oh! No." *Please ask me once more...please.*

"Remember your promise to have dinner with me? Let's have that tonight. Come on." He gesticulated to his driver to load her baggage into the car.

"Umm...okay." *Yippee!*

Sitting beside Haasil she could feel his leg hitting hers whenever the car wobbled on the uneven road. He wasn't aware of the touch but she was and for once she deliberately hit him. And immediately cursed herself. *What are you silly Jilly? Sixteen?* The car hit a sudden bumper and Haasil, for support, placed his hand on her thighs instead of the seat.

"I am really sorry." He apologized removing his hand quickly.

Does he remember he touched my thighs in the elevator once?

"It's okay."

A few minutes passed by. The streets were flooded with people, vehicle and smoke. There was no respite anywhere. *Should I wish him now?* As her mind vacillated she heard Haasil speak.

"What happened to your dad?"

"He is a diabetes patient and was suddenly taken ill. Was in the hospital for a day but now is at home doing fine."

"That's good." He was about to say more when his mobile rang. "Excuse me." He picked up the call. "Yes darling."

Swadha gave a confused glance at Haasil. *Darling? Who the hell on earth is he talking to?*

"Ya I am on my way dear. And I have a guest with me. You'll get to know when I reach home."

"Love you." Swadha heard the female voice say.

"Ya." Haasil sounded a little uncomfortable. "Same here." A soft confession.

"See you."

The moment the call ended Haasil turned towards Swadha, "Didn't tell her about you. She'll be pleasantly surprised."

"Who are you talking about?" Swadha's heart had already started throbbing. *He has already got another woman?*

"Palki, who else? She is waiting for us!"

For few seconds nothing made any sense. And some words, suddenly, started playing an out-of-sync orchestra within her. *Haasil is serious and his wife is presumed dead. His wife is presumed dead. Wife is presumed dead. Presumed dead. Dead!* Those were the exact words of Amit, the head of corporate strategy at NH Consultants. Did he lie to me? Oh shit! Oh heaven shit! Now, when I have patiently knitted the complete sweater of my dreams, it's suddenly summer! Can't be! She felt like standing on the terrace of preparation helplessly watching the airplane of opportunity fly high above only to vanish into the clouds of reality. Must be a joke! But why would he crack such a sadist joke? Of course he knows how much I love him. I mean I haven't told him yet but can't he read my eyes, my body language...my heart? Why would Amit lie to me? Or, is Haasil lying to me now?

"And don't worry Palki likes you a lot!" She heard Haasil say.

He sure is kidding, she concluded.

Silly Jilly! He is not – Swadha didn't care to listen.

The house seemed quiet from outside. As the car came to a slow halt beside the lawn Swadha observed the curtains were all shut tight and no source of light was visible inside the house. *There isn't anyone inside. There cant be. There shouldn't be.* Swadha prayed on.

The moment Haasil kept his finger on the calling bell the door opened up. He exchanged an anxious glance with Swadha. Instead of pressing the bell he pushed the door instead. With his first step touching the floor the lights were switched on and there were jubilant claps coming from different corner along with the typical 'happy birthday' song played by a stereo. For a moment Haasil didn't move. He only panned his eyes from Nitin to Sanjana to Amit to Raima, Amit's fiancée, to Pallavi. With a red strapless gown, veiling her from bust to feet, a svelte hair cut and a shinning diamond pendant, giving her the aura of a complete woman, Pallavi looked the most beautiful he had seen her thus far.

She walked up to him and kissed his cheeks. There was another minor round of claps. "Happy birthday sweetheart!" She said presenting him a red rose.

"Oh!" Acute happiness blocked Haasil's flow of words.

"Thanks!" He soon blurted out, kissed Pallavi back and hugged her. As she inhaled his odour Pallavi felt supremely alive. She smiled to herself but it quickly dried down as her eyes fell on Swadha who, standing behind Haasil, was waiting to enter the house.

Haasil loosened the hug and said, "Jesus! One helluva of a surprise!" He noticed Pallavi was looking behind him. He turned. "Oh! I am sorry. I got Swadha mid way and invited her here." Pallavi and Nitin exchanged a quick glance as Haasil tried to explain, "I didn't know there was a party-"

"Hey!" Nitin cut him short. "It's good that you brought her along." He nudged Sanjana. "Yes" She spoke, "now women will be in majority!" Everyone smiled at Swadha.

"Hi." Pallavi sounded cold, "Please do come in." And icy.

Swadha didn't get a chance to talk to Haasil again during the party.

The giant cake, oozing mouth-watering cream from every corner, was cut within few minutes of his arrival. The first piece he cut out was lovingly offered to Pallavi who put half of it into Haasil's mouth and then took a bite from there. That called for a collective 'ooo' from the others.

"So sweet!" Sanjana commented.

"Ya." Swadha wanted to throw up. She felt humiliatingly manipulated. Though she knew this wasn't Palki but her senses proved it otherwise. The excuse that she would soon talk to Amit for clarifications momentarily calmed the storm of confusion inside her. But half an hour into the party it still remained only a desire. The men hooked themselves near the bar corner while the ladies, sitting on the sofa, were discussing nothing in particular.

"Hey Swadha you are not saying *kuch bhi*?" Raima, oblivious to every latent aspect, said aloud.

"Sorry?" She averted her eyes from Haasil to Raima.

"How is office going?"

"Fine."

"You are the serious types *kya*? I *toh* can't keep quiet for a single second *baba*!"

"Aren't you feeling comfortable?" It was Pallavi. She looked straight at Swadha who, since the time she saw her, read pure contempt in her eyes.

"No, actually I had a hectic travel so-"

"Why don't you drink something? Orange or cola?"

Palki was hundred times more sober and without any attitude....but then why is this fake Palki here?

"Orange." Swadha had a plan.

Pallavi looked at the table and said, "Oops! Gotta fetch some!" She went to the kitchen calling Raghu *chacha's* name while Swadha, triggered by impatience, followed her. Nitin only noticed the endeavour from the bar corner without being kinetic.

Pausing near the kitchen Swadha observed the scene inside. She saw Pallavi explaining something to the cook who was filling an empty glass with *Fanta*. He wanted to bring the glass but Pallavi took it from him and was about to step out when Swadha confronted her.

"Oh! I would have got you the glass there."

"Never mind." Swadha faked a smile. "It's a long time we met, isn't?"

"Ya." *Is she testing me?* "Ya!"

"You remember how I stumbled last time and fell on you?" Swadha sounded hyper.

Pallavi took time. "Oh! Yes that surely was some scene! Come let's join the others." Pallavi said marching on.

She is not Palki, Swadha was confident now. There was no stumbling episode whatsoever. *What's up with the real Palki? If she is dead then Haasil should know about it and if she is not then where the hell is she anyways? And who is this with whom Haasil is so happy?*

During the rest of the party Swadha's eyes kept following Pallavi. They registered the smallest details each time with a sublime knock on the door of her realization: she was not Palki. *No way!*

She wanted to talk to Amit but Raima's non-sense chirps never gave her that space. Talking to Nitin was out of question for she never was frank with him. The irritation of not being able to talk to Amit kept her quiet for most of the time adhering to only one word reply whenever a necessity poked her. Finally, with reluctance written all over her face, she chose to wait till the next day in office.

Faking a headache, immediately after dinner, Swadha took leave. As promised Haasil's driver dropped her at her place.

The moment she unlocked her door, dragged her luggage in, locked the door again and surrendered herself on the small chair she started sobbing. Loneliness, sometimes, stabs exactly where it hurts the most and with what penetrates the most: failure.

Yes, that's what she thought of herself as. A failure! First Rajesh, then Soham and now Haasil. Different reasons, same result.

Don't worry silly Jilly. At least you were honest with your feelings with all the three. But what did I get being honest? *There's no set formula in love. You get it or you don't – simple!* But why it is only the latter with me? Was it my fault that Rajesh was gay? No! But I had to pay for it! Was it my fault Soham's mother had committed to someone else? No! But I had to pay for it. *I understand silly Jilly but…* I am not a computer, I am a human being. I can't format my heart each time a love virus contaminates it. I can't forget everything even if I want to. Some hurts always stay. No matter how much I presume the next relationship might be the one I am born for God devises some funny excuses to get me out of it. *Calm down silly Jilly.* After Soham I had promised myself not to fall in love till my parents choose someone for me but when I saw Haasil I thought…Swadha broke down further. Her breaths became long…I thought I might as well give one last shot but I turned out to be third time unlucky. *Love is weird darling and people who expect love to behave normally are weirdos.* Look at that fake woman! She is cheating Haasil and still God is allowing her to live, laugh and sleep with Haasil. *Remember silly Jilly what mom said: no bane, no gain.* She brought her purse near and opened it for tissue papers. She took one out and was about to wipe her tears when she realized it wasn't a tissue. It was a piece of paper with a note that read:

Forget him else you'll lose your job.

All the remorse, as Swadha read the note for few more times, transformed into an uncompromising wrath.

"Why did you write that?" Nitin was utterly cross with Pallavi. It was well past midnight and they were talking over the phone.

"I felt like!" Pallavi pitch was low. She was in the hall while Haasil was asleep in his room.

"You felt like? Who do you think you are?"

"Haasil's wife."

"Look Pallavi you know the situation is fragile. We have to move ahead with utmost care. Now what if Swadha confides everything to Haasil?"

"What'll she tell him?"

"It can be anything. She had met Palki once. Who knows, may be by now she already knows you aren't her."

"Why don't you just chuck her out of the company?"

"It's not a *pan* shop that I run. She is vital for the company's growth. We can't afford to lose her. Why the hell didn't you ask me before writing that shit?"

"You have already said it twice."

"I'll say it for the rest of the night if I want to!"

"I love Haasil and I can't tolerate any second woman."

"Second woman? Who told you she is a second woman?"

"She loves him. I know."

"If you know that then don't forget you too are a second woman."

"Haasil loves *me!*"

"You aren't sure of that yet. And if you really want that to happen some day then stop behaving like a fool. If tomorrow Swadha talks about the note to Haasil then...shit! How carefully I had planned everything…all shall be ruined."

"I don't care."

"You don't care? If you loved Haasil then you wouldn't have said this. And what is it you don't care? Haasil or your love for him? For let me tell you if you continue to be like this then your stupidity will affect both, sooner or later."

Pallavi didn't reply though Nitin could hear her rapid breathing.

"I am sorry."

"It's not the time to be sorry. It's time to think what to do if Haasil gets to know about the note." There was a lull-before-a-storm kind of tension in his voice. "But before that just pray he doesn't get to know about it by any means."

Though Haasil woke up late but, with Pallavi's help, he made it on time to office. I don't know what I would have done without her, he wondered, as he settled on the chair in his private office room switching on his Macbook. While it loaded he made a quick call to Pallavi to inform her he had reached office safely.

For the next half hour he perused all the notes made during the business tour. He wanted to consult Nitin and Amit on some points. Without taking his eyes away from the laptop he picked up the intercom and was about to dial his secretary when he heard a knock on the door.

"Come in."

"Good morning sir."

"Good morning Neha. I was about to call you." He kept the receiver down.

She gave a full thirty-two out smile in response and said, "Swadha Kashyap left this for you sir."

"Swadha?" A glimmer of curiosity was visible in his reaction.

"Yes, this morning."

"Okay."

Neha went away. Haasil tore open the envelope and pulled out the letter inside. He read it with a bewildered face.

Swadha has resigned? But she didn't tell me anything yesterday. He dialled her mobile but it was switched off. *What happened overnight? Or was she planning it for a long time? Nitin said she was an asset to the company. Does he know?*

His thoughts were interrupted by a knock again.

"Yes."

"Sorry sir" it was Neha again, "I forgot this DVD."

"DVD?"

"It's addressed to you."

"Did it arrive this morning too?"

"No, yesterday."

"Thanks. Could you please ask Nitin to come here once."

"Sure sir." She walked away.

Haasil opened the brown envelop and took out the DVD. Something was written with a red marker. It read: 'You think you know about your wife?'

Now what's this? Haasil tried not to jump to any inauspicious conclusion. He played the DVD in his laptop.

As the video ran a man was seen setting up a wobbling camera on its tripod. When it was done he moved to the bed where a woman was...Palki! Haasil jumped to the edge of his seat and immediately turned off the video. What. The. Fucking. Hell.

He had been shot. No, he had been stabbed. Yes, he had been both shot and stabbed right at his heart. The different parts of his body had their own weird way of reacting to the unbelievably vulgar sight. He could feel his laboured heart beats which, like a train approaching a terminal station, were slowing down. The limbs started to tremble beyond control. The lungs felt seriously choked and thus could expand only slightly. The guts, abruptly, were contracting themselves which made him, for once, want to throw out even his breakfast.

With trembling hands he played the video again this time from the middle. The man was ploughing her mercilessly. Her eyes were closed and legs were around his hips with her hands caressing his back. And the worst: she was seemingly enjoying all of it.

Haasil couldn't watch it for more than five seconds. He scampered to the attached toilet with his hand on his mouth and threw up in the wash basin. He wanted to vomit all the nettlesome feelings out, as well, but they already had become too deep a part of him to come out easily.

"Hey, where are you buddy?"

Haasil wiped his eyes when he heard Nitin. "I am in here."

"Ok! I am waiting."

"Sure." Haasil washed his face quickly, dried it with the towel and took one deep breath looking at his punctured image in the mirror. I'll have to talk it over with Palki before anybody else gets to know about it.

"I am sorry Nitin. I have an upset stomach. I think I'll go home."

"You sure should. I'll ask the doctor to-"

Haasil raised his hand, "No need. I only need some rest." He sounded suspiciously grave.

"Are you sure?"

Haasil replied only after he had put the Macbook in its case. "I am."
He left Nitin with an alert mind, "Something is wrong." His eyes fell
on Swadha's resignation. He read it out and mumbled under his breath,
"Something *surely* is wrong."

He dialled Pallavi's number.

Once in his car Haasil asked his driver to take him to an open place
first and fast. He drove him to Marine Drive.

It was raining intermittently. Mumbai rains are tantamount to life's
problems. Once it starts it simply keeps pouring and pouring. As Haasil
got out of his car the driver warned him once of the rain, "*Saab baarish.*"
But he didn't care.

Except for a few couples using umbrellas to hide themselves from
the world the place was lonely. Haasil came close to the cemented
boundary and stood there with his emotions coalescing with nature's.
The latter was soaking the earth below whereas the former was soaking
the earth of his belief inside. *Was everything a lie? Was every goddamn
thing fake?*

The scene from the video flashed in his mind. Nausea, again, caught
up with him. *Was it a one night fling or a prolonged affair? The man is
Indian but they did it here in my absence or in her University? But why did
she have to do it? If she likes him more than me she could have told me once
– just once – and I wouldn't even have asked for any explanation. I can't
believe this! In the last two-three months she had been lying to me with a
straight face! And not for a single second did I feel she didn't love me! And
who knows may be she was trying to cheat me before the accident too! As he*

ran his, still jittery, fingers through his wet hair he suddenly felt heavy. His suit was soaking wet. *Shit!* He mumbled to himself. *Shit!* He yelled at the open space in front. It called for few curious glances from the scattered public. Haasil was quick to regain his composure but a second later, compulsively, kicked the cement boundary hard. It hurt! *Not more than...*

"*Saab.*" He turned to see the driver running towards him.

"Phone." He gave him the mobile and hopped back to the car.

The caller's name read Palki.

"Hey dear. Where are you? Nitin told me you are coming back home. What happened?"

"I am on my way." His voice sounded pre-programmed. "Shall talk then." He pressed the end call option.

Let's see what she has to say about it. A minute after staring blankly at the sky, which resembled a beggar's stitched blanket with the patches of black clouds, Haasil made a dash for his car.

From the time Nitin had called her Pallavi carried a constant knot of an obnoxious premonition in her stomach. *I'm not having a good feeling about today.* And the knot only tightened when Haasil ended the call abruptly. With impatience riding on her Pallavi sauntered across the hall to open the door when the sound of the engine of a car, coming to a halt, hit her ears.

She smiled seeing Haasil coming out of the car. *Oh! He is totally drenched!* "What happened? How did you get wet?" She asked him as he walked past her — with null reaction — to head straight for the stairs. Her smile vanished with Haasil disappearing into the bedroom. Pallavi closed the door behind him and ambled towards the staircase with unsure steps.

By the time she reached the corridor, she could hear vulgar moans escaping the bedroom. *What is he doing?* And as she stepped inside her eyes not only fell on the forty-inch LCD television screen framed on the wall, facing the bed, but also on the porn flick it played.

"What's this?" She saw the DVD player was on.

Haasil, sitting on the edge of the bed, forwarded the video with the remote and paused on a frame that showed Pallavi's face clearly. He turned and asked, "What's this Palki?"

Pallavi's lips – very slowly – parted in disbelief. She felt the volcano of fear erupting inside her. The truth of the moment dwarfed all her nightmares. *Thomas! How did he find Haasil?*

"Who" She stammered, "Who gave you this?"

"First tell me" Haasil shouted standing up, "what the fuck is this?" He flung the remote at the television.

What should I tell him? What all should I tell him? Pallavi silently stared at the two broken pieces of the remote.

"What are you quiet for? Why did you lie that you love me? Huh?" His rage directed his constant up and down pacing.

"I didn't lie that I love you."

"Then what's this? Your proof?"

"It's not what you think."

"Then what is it? Tell me, I want to know. Or do you think I don't have the right."

"Please! You have every right. Okay let me tell you. This guy had drugged me into it. If you see the video carefully and calmly you'll see I don't open my eyes at all." This was the truth. "He tried to blackmail me earlier also but I didn't let him. And now he is back." The first lie.

"What is his name?"

"Thomas."

"When did this happen?"

"A few years back."

"Why didn't you tell me this before?"

"I thought he was gone from my life."

"Did I know about it before the accident?"

"Yes." The second lie.

"What did we do to tackle him then?"

"Gave him some money." The third lie.

"But this time I have a better plan." Haasil reached for his suit lying at the other end of the bed. He searched the pocket and took out his cell.

"What are you going to do?"

"Inform the police."

Shit! "No, don't inform the police."

Haasil paused and looked intently at her. Pallavi averted her eyes looking pathetically shaky.

"Why?" It was a cold voiced query.

No answer.

"Why shouldn't I inform the police?"

The fucking truth will be out then. I anyways will tell you everything but give me some time Haasil...it won't be good for our future if the truth comes out this way, Pallavi's mind pleaded. It was the same Pallavi who – once upon a time – had an excuse for all the matters of head and heart.

"Bad name!"

"What?"

"If we involve the police it would bring in the media. And then our names, your company's name everything will-"

"I don't give a damn." He pushed her aside and walked out of the room with his cell.

"Haasil wait."

He turned around standing by the first step of the staircase, "Once more you stop me and I'll assume you are not telling me the complete truth." He started again.

"Haasil…"

This time he paused on the third step and turned around slowly. *So the truth is something else.*

"I was right damn it." He was appalled. "The truth is that he is your lover, isn't it?"

"No, he isn't."

He gave her a you-are-impossible look. "Ya, Sure!" He climbed down the stairs indifferently.

The truth or another lie – it was Hobson's choice for Pallavi. Either ways, her guts told her, she wouldn't be able to avoid her life from getting screwed up. May be only this time it will be irreversibly so. She never prayed for a win at anything and yet, all her life Pallavi had been winning – this way or that. But the one time she prayed Pallavi found herself on the very edge of her much sought after world with the depth of an once-in-a-lifetime kind of failure staring at her. She rubbed her eyes watching Haasil sit on the couch, downstairs, with resignation. As if he had already put the whole truth in his context and was content with it. And even if he wasn't, Haasil didn't look interested anymore.

I'll tell the truth and he would respect me for coming out with it. He might be rude with me for a few days but then he'll be alright. After all I didn't kill Palki nor is she alive. He'll have to come to me in the end. And I'll

*win him forever. Yes that's the way it's going to be. I will win. Not Palki.
Pallavi will win. Like always.*

"I am not Palki."

She yelled in rebellion to her destiny more than anything else.

"Now what?" Nitin barked at the driver.

"Signal again sir."

All the traffic signals of the city, it seemed, were throwing their
attitude at his car displaying their red avatar at every crossing. "Bullshit."
He slammed his hand on the driver's seat.

But that was only an excuse to vent his frustration. *Everything was
going so damn smooth but for Pallavi's stupidity last night. I am sure Swadha
must have shown Haasil the note. Fuck shit.*

After what seemed like a journey to old age Nitin finally reached his
destination. He hurried out of the car and almost ran for the door bell.

Raghu, with his typical servility, opened the door at the first bell.

"*Chacha aap* please *bahar rahiye.*" Nitin requested. He didn't want
him to hear anything. Raghu, glancing once at his *Saab* and *memsaab's*
gloomy face, obliged. He closed the door from outside.

Seeing the two sitting far apart Nitin couldn't control his curiosity
any long.

"Now will you guys tell me what has happened?"

Haasil gave him a blank stare and said, "Ask Pallavi."

Nitin turned towards Pallavi and in a flash towards his friend again.
Good Lord! He knows. Holyshit!

Pallavi, bereft of emotions, told Nitin about the DVD and Thomas.

The information was new for him too. And he was shocked to say the least. Nobody spoke for the next one hour. They simply sat at their respective places desperately wishing for time to breeze away and a happy solution to come up on its own. They, in their own perspective, wanted some magic to act on the reality and make it unreal.

Haasil suddenly stood up and fetched himself a cold bottle of water from the refrigerator in the kitchen. He drank some water. Still, his thirst wasn't quenched. He drank some more. Still the same. *No amount of water will be able to push the gruesome truth inside me.*

"I am sorry Palki!" Haasil banged the bottle on the dining table. "I am sorry. I loved you Palki. I love only you." And he kept banging the bottle till the plastic went out of shape. Nitin scampered to him and held both his hands from behind. Haasil furiously tried to break free. "Leave me. I don't want to live. I killed my wife." But Nitin held on tight. "It was an accident damn it!" He yelped back.

"No I killed her. Not only killed her but insulted her love for me by sleeping with another woman."

"Calm down. You didn't do anything. Cool it now. Cool." He held him steady till both their breathing reached the plateau of normalcy.

Since the time she narrated the turn of events to Nitin, and also all throughout the little scuffle, Pallavi remained indifferently quiet. As if she wasn't present in the room at all. She was sitting on one of the sofas, staring at the ceiling with the demeanour of total surrender, with tears, like tourists, constantly rolling out to visit her cheeks and lips. She wished to explain many things. And wanted to start from the time she was a teenager. But each time a thought occurred her senses set it aside as pointless.

Nitin, in the meantime, helped Haasil sit on one of the dining chairs and was himself back on the sofa. "I am sorry – I am really sorry

Haasil." He was looking at Haasil who dug his face on his arms spread on the table. From the subtle tremors his body suffered Nitin knew he was sobbing profusely.

"I can't explain what went through me when I heard Palki and you had met with an accident. When I was told Palki's body was missing I had a gut feeling it was for the worse."

"Missing?" Haasil lifted his head to look at his friend inquiringly.

"Ya. We still don't have her dead body. Though the police are on the lookout but nothing encouraging has happened thus far."

"What do you mean you haven't got her dead body?"

"The people who found you didn't see her body."

"That means she is alive." He stood up with a sudden pizzazz.

"Everything from the newspaper to the detective agency has been tried. No success."

The ember of hope extinguished. Haasil, sitting down slowly, dug his face again in his arms as Nitin continued.

"When I saw you opening your eyes in the hospital I felt alive myself. But when I learnt from the doctor that you'd have memory problems I was sad and happy at the same time. I don't have to clarify on my sadness but I was happy because that way you wouldn't enquire about Palki. Not immediately at least. And slowly I thought I would let you know of the truth. But one day you happened to see Palki's picture following which came my first lie to you. That she is still alive. Believe me *yaar* I wanted to tell you the truth but it simply refused to come out." Nitin choked on the last segment. "And every other lie is only a ramification of that one lie. So it's not really Pallavi's fault. It's mine."

"God damn it!" Haasil banged the table once and looked at Nitin. "If the bugger had not delivered this DVD then I would have never known the truth. I would have continued to love someone as my wife who, in reality, doesn't love me at all."

The last words broke Pallavi's zombie-like trance. She looked at Haasil and said, "I love you Haasil. I *really* do. Please believe me." She almost begged. Something which was unprecedented with her. But so was being the real Pallavi after years of existence.

"Believe you?" Pallavi had excited the lava of frustration in him. "Nobody, who claims to be in love, can lie to her love with locked eyes. Or otherwise."

"I would have eventually told you everything."

"Don't even try that nonsense."

"No, she really would have done that for she loves you."

"So? What should I do if she loves me? That's none of my business. I love only my wife. And that's Palki. Holyhell Nitin! You made me sleep with another woman!"

"People do that these days anyways! That's no issue. And nobody forced her."

"I don't do that. I am married for God's sake!"

"But Palki is dead." Pallavi poured in.

"What if she is dead? Just because someone is dead it doesn't mean he becomes past tense. And if I decide to assign my whole life, my mind, heart and soul to my Palki do you have any problem? Do you?" He howled at both.

"All these months you have loved me. Only me!"

"I think you didn't get me. I. Love. Palki. No one else." His eyes were naked of mercy.

"But why aren't you giving me a chance?" Pallavi retorted. "Why do you think I left my job, my family and decided to play your wife? Would have I done that if I didn't love you? You think that's easy? You think any girl can do that easily?"

"Oh! So now you are proud of what you did! Great!"

Pallavi shot a helpless look but still tried to make her point clear to Haasil, "I understand how painful it is for you but please, for heaven's sake, understand my position too. I surrendered every inch of my existence playing your wife."

"So do you want me to sympathize and cooperate with you because you happened to play my wife in the last few months? By the way, what exactly do you want? That I too play your husband for the rest of the life? Bullshit!"

"Listen Haasil." Nitin tried to step in.

"Please." Haasil shot his hand at him. "You'd your chance. I would have preferred you telling me the truth in the beginning itself. It would have killed me for sure but wouldn't have turned me into a living dead like its doing now. Tell me have you left me with anything to look forward to in life?"

Nitin restrained himself.

"You have me Haasil." Pallavi got up and moved towards him. She sat down grasping his hand. "You still have me."

"No, I don't need you anymore."

"Please don't talk like that. I love you like mad and can't afford to lose you. I promise with time you'll forget Palki and accept me."

"Forget Palki?" He freed his hand of her grasp. "Firstly I don't have any intention of doing that. And secondly, with you here in this house my wounds will never heal and also I shall hate myself for you'll remind me how I have cheated Palki."

"Cheated?"

"Marriage, for me, is the promise of love. I am not sure whether it'll make sense to you or not but you've, in a way, pushed me to pollute that promise. And I'll never forgive you for that. Never ever."

"But I did what Nitin wanted me to do. I didn't have any interest of my own."

"Don't kid me. Nitin lied because he wanted to see me happy. His lies hurt me alright. But your lies have violated my feelings for Palki and manipulated my thoughts."

"I can't believe this! I am telling you my lies were a part of Nitin's lies. Why aren't you getting me?"

"Did he ask you to say yes to his proposal of playing my wife? No! Bloody no. You said yes to that stupid idea of his because it was fulfilling your teenage-born desire of getting me. Winning me rather! You did it because you wanted to live happily with me. It didn't matter if the process affected my faith for somebody. You did it because you thought you could design your life to your liking using me. Even if it meant blasting my love for someone else into pieces. You said yes because you are a pathetic coward. You didn't have the courage to stand as Pallavi in front of me. That's why the garb of Palki. You thought once I am in love with you – assuming you to be my wife – you would leave me no option but to carry on. Let me tell you that's pure bullshit! People like you live only to satisfy their selfish interests doesn't matter if it ruins other people of their precious possession. Yes maybe we all do that at some point or the other but you...you guys do *only* that. Nothing else. And for every shit of yours you have only one excuse: love! God damn you."

Pallavi remained quiet.

"You told me that you loved me for so many years. But you know what? If you really loved me you should have come in my life as Pallavi and not Palki whatever be my situation. Firstly, because you don't have the worth to be Palki and secondly, you can never be Palki. Not even in your thoughts.

If you really loved me you could have explained the situation to me. I would have cried and wished I was dead but I still would have respected you. Now nothing can happen between the two of us. Absolutely nothing. And now I want you to leave this place and my life immediately. I don't care whether someone is blackmailing you or not. I simply don't give a goddamn fuck."

Haasil got up and headed furiously towards the door.

"Hey bro, listen! Let's take it slowly. You are being too fast with your decision. Let us decide everything once your anger dissolves."

"If you want to wait till my anger dissolves then you'll waste your life." He walked out of the house and came back few seconds later.

"And Nitin if you are really my friend and want me to pardon you for the rubbish that you planned up then by the time I return I want her to move out of my house."

"Where are you-" Nitin started but Haasil was gone before he could complete.

Once in the lawn he shouted at the driver who left his filmy gossip with Raghu and the security guard and ran clumsily to bring out the car.

"Where to sir?"

Haasil didn't have a clue. The only two persons he knew and trusted were the ones he had left in his house. "Do you remember where you'd dropped Swadha on the party night?" It was an impulse he was acting on.

"Swadha ma'am? Versova."

"Take me there."

"Who gave you the DVD? Nitin howled at Pallavi the moment Haasil walked off. "And why the hell did you not tell me about these things before?"

"I am talking to you Pallavi." He shook her holding her shoulders. "Speak up now."

"Why didn't you tell me this before? You knew we were walking on razor's edge, didn't you?"

"Haasil is right. I was blinded by an illusion. The illusion that I can manipulate life according to my liking. Instead, I got manipulated. There were few things in my life to which I never gave any second thoughts. Not when I was doing them at least. But after I met Haasil again I – on my own – died so many deaths within myself in order to change all that. To change my past! On one hand I didn't want to take a single chance risking a separation with him and on the other – may be unknowingly – I kept preparing the ground only for that." She looked at Nitin, "If I'd told you these earlier you wouldn't have allowed me to be his wife."

Nitin slowly bowed his head agreeing with the fact.

"It was tough for me lying point blank everyday. I cursed myself for that. But still I held onto a wan faith that one day when I'll tell him the details he would love me because of my love and respect for him. But now-" She got up and, with heavy steps, proceeded towards the stairs.

"Where are you going?"

"There are a lot of things to be packed."

"Are you really going to leave?"

Pallavi didn't respond. She turned around once after the climbing the stairs. "Can something be done about Thomas?"

"If I don't crack open his ass I won't call myself Nitin Punjabi anymore." Nitin's eyes read vengeance.

"Thanks Nitin. You know what? Whenever I have done things on instincts I've been always right. Remember, I told you this won't work out and sooner or later Haasil would come to know about it. But when you showed me his photograph I dared my instinct, probably, for the only time in my life." Anytime now, she was positive, an emotional intercourse would begin between nostalgia and premonitions at the end of which she would be left drained of life. "Though I know I shouldn't have done that...shouldn't have asked you for the photograph...shouldn't have said yes bypassing all issues like a fool but still I will continue to be proud of my foolishness for the rest of my life or whatever that is left."

Pallavi disappeared into the bedroom leaving a wet-eyed Nitin down in the hall. Inside, she cried without full-stop for almost an hour after which she started packing. When she was done she decided to leave a letter for Haasil. She went to the study, took one of his writing pads and sat down to write.

Dear Dino

(I know this name upsets you but it's the same name which has shown me the heaven like side of life.)

I might as well have told you whatever I am going to write now but I guess hiding behind paper gives me the necessary strength to stand in the court of guilt. More so because I already know the verdict.

I stand by what I have told you before. Whatever you now know about me is true. Absolutely. It was me in the video. I have never been to any foreign university. I am not married to you and most importantly I am not Palki. You were right I can never be like her. But more than that I want to know what I should do to deserve what she deserves: that's you. I hope to know the secret some day or may be some life.

Don't worry I won't use this letter to plant any sapling of mercy in you. Instead I would use the space to let you know about few secrets between my heart and soul. I would also not ask you to believe whatever I write but would definitely plead you to go through the letter once.

Yes, many men have made me climax but when I said 'I love you' to you those pleasures were nothing in comparison. Each time you held me in your arms my whole existence felt pure from those deep and secluded corners in me which makes me a woman. My mom had once told me that the road that leads to a temple is difficult. It tests you, challenges you and many times beats your will. That's why few get to the Temple for which they were born. And when I saw you again – thanks to Nitin – I knew my hard, and to an extent treacherous journey, had ended. I – who once strongly adhered to 'sab chalta hai' attitude towards life – was ashamed of myself and my deeds. So many things could have been avoided. But by then, as the cliché goes, it was too late. Fate adds salt, our mistakes add pepper. That's how life gets its taste but I guess the pepper part was overdone by me.

Few people have understood me throughout my life. The general perception is I am arrogant and stubborn. But nobody ever cared to empathize with those undefined voids inside me which were thirsty for attention. I don't blame anyone for even I didn't care to understand the real me. Till I met you again, that is. Thanks for making me realize the importance of being oneself. Of course, to be oneself we have to, at first, know ourselves well. And to know the person within one has to fall in love.

The first time you touched my body with the warmth of passion and took me on a journey of a lifetime, I realized: love gives voice to our soul. And when you hugged me tight, after we were sapped of energy, the God inside me woke up. He injected guilt in me. I swear I would have told you everything eventually but my love-struck heart forgot the deadliest poison for a relationship is a lie. Several men have tried to make me feel special and appreciated me and my traits only to spread my legs. But you are the only one who showed me how bad I am. Thanks again.

Tell me, do we remember the day we are born? Likewise neither do I remember the day I fell in love with you. It might have been the first day I saw you fifteen years ago or the day I met you again fifteen years later. Or, perhaps anytime in-between. I believe most of us remain a bud all our lives, with an impoverished hope of embracing, one day, what the world has to offer, and perhaps die being likewise. But there are few who get touched by the ethereal hand of love and finally flower. I am glad you gave my interior a chance to flower.

I won't say I'll miss you. For that'll be a gross lie. How can we miss our heartbeats? We can always feel it, right inside our core. I don't know what I'll do now. But I'm sure of two things: I am not killing myself and I am not coming back to you again. I am not a coward to do the former and I don't have the courage to do the latter. I might have to marry someone but you see there can be many moons but there is, and will always be, only one Sun. And one who has spent more than half of her life bathing in the Sun no other form of light can ever enlighten her. Above all I know very well no matter how many men come in my life from now on your memories will be more significant, relevant and important than any of their physical presence.

Take care and all the best in the life ahead…I never wanted this to end this way but…never mind…irrespective of whatever happened each spool of my prayer would always be for you and each cry of my soul would be earning for your well being. My life from now on will be like a newspaper featuring only the headlines of despair and heartaches. No problem as along with every other news yours will always be there…

Lastly, my destiny gave me your name and made you my first love. Now, I have given back your name to destiny and said you are my last love. And *this time I'll win because to beat Pallavi one should have her permission!*

Your's, (in my own way)

Pallavi.

She kept staring at the letter for sometime and then tore it to pieces. "No need of this shit." She smiled helplessly and cried again.

When Pallavi finally came down to the hall with her luggage she noticed Nitin still sitting there.

"Where are you going?" He asked.

"I'll take the first flight to Delhi. Could you arrange for a ticket?"

"Are you sure? Every decision need not be taken in the spur of the moment. If you could wait then may be with time…"

"Time can only heal wounds not amputations."

Nitin thought for a while and said, "Alright. If you want I can talk to the airlines to absorb you in their payroll again."

"That won't be necessary." There was a strange stubbornness in her voice.

On her way from New Delhi's Indira Gandhi Airport to her father's place, later in the evening, Pallavi called her mother.

"Hello mom." It was after three years she was talking to her. And her mother instantly broke down hearing her voice.

"Pallo! Where are you beta? I missed you a lot."

"I too missed you mom. And papa too." She somehow managed not to bias her voice with the pain inside.

"I am coming home within few minutes. I am in Delhi. Tell me mom does papa's friend still wants me as his daughter-in-law?"

"He does."

"I am ready mom. I have lived my life enough."

And now its time to experience death.

When the driver stopped the car right in front of Swadha's apartment Haasil only had to ask the guard to locate her flat. It was Swadha who opened the door.

"The bathroom is that way." She had almost turned her back when Haasil spoke, "Sorry?"

The voice punctuated her motion and she turned around in a flash to realize it was not the plumber.

"Haasil?"

"I am sorry to come like this. But can I spend sometime at your place?"

Sometime? Swadha stood still. *Say yes silly Jilly!*

"Oh yes." She smiled through her bloodshot swollen eyes.

"What made you resign?" It was the first thing he asked after making himself comfortable on a plastic chair.

Swadha, instead of replying, preferred showing him Pallavi's note. *Should I tell him the truth? But what if it angers him?*

"I apologize for this."

Swadha was quiet.

"And I'll think you have forgiven me only if you join NH Consultants again."

"But what if your wife objects again. I can't take it-"

"She is not my wife."

Oh! He knows! "I know that."

Haasil looked at her, surprised.

She explained him her part. Then he explained his. By the time he was out of her place he had convinced Swadha to join the company again.

Closing the door behind her Swadha smiled to herself. After almost forty hours of crying.

Now he is not only single but your friend too! And what did that movie say? A man and a woman can never be friends! Silly Jilly you rock! A funny chill ran through all the *wrong* parts. She hit her head softly, blushing.

The Times of India, after five days, carried the headlines: BLUE FILM RACKET BUSTED BY MUMBAI POLCIE. CITY'S LEADING DJ INVOLVED.

The same week a *Havan* was performed at Haasil's residence in Palki's name. There he met her parents for the first time after the accident. And when he learnt they never went on any spiritual trip his disgust for Pallavi only scaled up.

Haasil didn't let his personal debacle to interfere with his professional developments. Though, personally, he turned a little cold towards Nitin but in the office his professional tempo was maintained. *If Pallavi is guilty then so is he. How can a successful entrepreneur be so foolish? Emotion does strange things to the best of brains.* Still, he thought he owed it to Nitin for whatever he did for him. *At least his intentions were to help me to get a life whereas Pallavi wanted to erase Palki from my existence. Whatever made her think that was possible!*

Nitin apologized several times but gave up, in the end, acknowledging Sanjana's words: Give him some time he'll definitely understand you.

A month later Haasil changed his house.

"I don't think I'll be able to live here." He confided to Nitin. "I am alone and I don't need that big a house anyways." He took a flat in Bandra.

As days passed Haasil chose business as his anodyne. Work became his salvation and the only obligation he was happy to have. He worked till late nights, avoided parties – official or otherwise – or get-togethers. He started touring a lot and within six months the change in his *modus vivendi* helped him somewhat deal with the tryst of destiny if not forget it completely. And amidst all the dark nights of reality the only morning of solace happened whenever he talked to his new found friend in the form of Swadha Kashyap.

They didn't go out on dates, never lunched together or hung around together. They rarely met outside office but every Saturday night they rang each other up. It was started by Swadha. The next Saturday, as if bound by an invisible understanding, Haasil did the same. And the endeavour continued. Technology gave them the optimum freedom of talking to the other with the necessary privacy of not having to do so eye to eye. Else some of their deep rooted emotions wouldn't have skimmed out.

"Its strange" he told her over the phone, "when you love someone in the presence of your wife the society talks about it and when you don't want to love anyone because your wife is dead the society still talks about it. Developing we are!"

The thermometer of her heart gave the maximum reading for respect.

"They still haven't found her dead body. Tell me do we see God? Still we try and keep our faith towards Him pure. I too want to keep my faith – that she'll return one day – alive in my heart."

"For how long?"

"I don't know. After all I too am only a human being and, may be, in the end I'll have to give in."

I'll wait for the end, Swadha promised herself.

"The fact that I have lost her doesn't hurt me as much as the fact that even after her demise I am continuing."

Sometime it was she who advised him.

"You see immediately after lunch we aren't interested in dinner but slowly, as the day progresses, we start feeling hungry." *Wow! Silly Jilly, you are the true descendent of Plato!*

"I guess you are right. What has happened has happened. No tears or prayer can change it."

Swadha invariably stretched her work to late nights only to get a glimpse of him whenever he called it a day finally. On one such late night she met him near the office entrance after work.

"Hey what are you doing here?"

"I am waiting for a cab."

"Oh! You never told me that before. It's risky for a girl to avail a cab this late. I can drop you whenever you get late."

Why else did I miss fives cabs for? "Won't that be a problem?"

"Remember we are friends outside office." He added.

"Thanks. But where's your car?"

"I had to park it a little far today. Come let's walk the distance together."

Walk the distance together! *Your time has sure begun silly Jilly!*

Epilogue

14th April.

The immediate year.

Hariharan, observing the woman from a distance, recollected part of his *Guruji's* words for the umpteenth time. *There will soon be a third person in your household and if you serve the person selflessly for exactly a year then you'll earn the blessings of God. He'll bless you with two sons and you'll live peacefully for the rest of your life and beyond. But remember it has to be selfless and for exactly one year.*

He had first seen the woman exactly a year back. Her body was an exhibition of wounds and her face was hardly identifiable with most part sustaining injury patches. He, for once, wondered if it would have been better if she was dead. But fate thought otherwise.

With Guruji's words beckoning his conscious Hariharan, owing to space problem in his vehicle, first took the woman to his forest hut from the accident spot. He was back by evening to fetch the man too but to his surprise the body had already been taken. That only reassured his faith in his Guruji. *You'll get to serve only one person.*

Initially the woman could neither talk nor move about. It was only on the seventh month that she finally started walking around with a wooden crunch. Hariharan had made it for her. He worked at a nearby forest reserve and was an artist with wood and a polymath about forest herbs. And with his knowledge he had made her breathe normally again.

The arrival of the woman made good luck kiss his destiny. His pay increased and he was also given a small one-room house to live along side his *babu's* bungalow. But he willfully forwent the opportunity. Only Hariharan knew how carefully he had kept the woman with him. There were policemen in the forest reserve itself and once he had seen her picture in a newspaper too but somehow, his Guruji's words, along with a lust for procuring a better life through the ritual of serving her, made him secure the secret.

Now that the desired time period was over Hariharan was upset. The flip in the chapters of time had made both Hariharan and his wife realize the strongest of all bonds are those that nature helps form between beings. They liked the woman but...

Reluctantly he went through his plan again – tomorrow I'll take her to the police and surrender. I'll tell them exactly why I had kept her for a year with me. As babu says *Satyamev Jayate*!

The thoughts were interrupted when his wife came up to him nervously.

"I helped her with her clothes today. And I saw something."

"What?"

"On her hips. Earlier it used to be vague because of the wounds but today-"

"Will you care to come out with it now?"

"There is something written beside her hips."

"What is it?"

"Its still not clear but something like...Palki-Haasil."

"Forget it. We'll surrender her to the police tomorrow. After that whatever they decide."